PUFFIN
A TASTE OF HEAVEN

MEG TILLY is the author of two YA novels, *Porcupine* and *First Time*. *Porcupine*—which was shortlisted for a BC Book Prize, the Canadian Library Association Best Children's Book, and for *Foreword* magazine's Book of the Year Award—was named an Ontario Library Top Ten Best Bet in 2008. *First Time* was a 2010 Canadian Children's Book Centre Best Book, a Golden Eagle Award nominee, and a 2009 YALSA Quick Pick. Her adult novels are *Singing Songs*—a Barnes & Noble Discover Great New Writers selection—and *Gemma*.

Tilly is also known for her work as a film actress. Some of her better-known films include *The Big Chill* and *Agnes of God*, for which she won a Golden Globe Award and was nominated for an Oscar.

At present she is both writing and dipping her toe back into the acting world. Recently, she played Martha in the Blue Bridge production of *Who's Afraid of Virginia Woolf?* and Madeline 2 in Tarragon Theatre's production of *The Real World?* As well, she is starring in Global TV's Canadian hit show *Bomb Girls*.

Tilly has three grown children and lives in Toronto with her husband.

meg tilly

a taste of heaven

PUFFIN
an imprint of Penguin Canada

Published by the Penguin Group
Penguin Group (Canada), 90 Eglinton Avenue East, Suite 700, Toronto, Ontario, Canada M4P 2Y3

Penguin Group (USA) Inc., 375 Hudson Street, New York, New York 10014, U.S.A.
Penguin Books Ltd, 80 Strand, London WC2R 0RL, England
Penguin Ireland, 25 St Stephen's Green, Dublin 2, Ireland (a division of Penguin Books Ltd)
Penguin Group (Australia), 707 Collins Street, Melbourne, Victoria 3008, Australia
(a division of Pearson Australia Group Pty Ltd)
Penguin Books India Pvt Ltd, 11 Community Centre, Panchsheel Park, New Delhi — 110 017, India
Penguin Group (NZ), 67 Apollo Drive, Rosedale, Auckland 0632, New Zealand
(a division of Pearson New Zealand Ltd)
Penguin Books (South Africa) (Pty) Ltd, 24 Sturdee Avenue, Rosebank,
Johannesburg 2196, South Africa

Penguin Books Ltd, Registered Offices: 80 Strand, London WC2R 0RL, England

First published 2013

1 2 3 4 5 6 7 8 9 10 (WEB)

Copyright © Meg Tilly, 2013

"Cheek To Cheek" by Irving Berlin
© Copyright 1935 by Irving Berlin
© Copyright Renewed
International Copyright Secured. All Rights Reserved. Reprinted by Permission.

Manufactured in Canada.

LIBRARY AND ARCHIVES CANADA CATALOGUING IN PUBLICATION

Tilly, Meg
A taste of heaven / Meg Tilly.

ISBN 978-0-14-318249-8

I. Title.

PS8589.I54T38 2013   jC813'.54   C2012-907537-X

Visit the Penguin Canada website at **www.penguin.ca**

Special and corporate bulk purchase rates available; please see
www.penguin.ca/corporatesales or call 1-800-810-3104, ext. 2477.

ALWAYS LEARNING   PEARSON

1
new girl

"Well, what do you know," Madison's dad said, his hand sliding out from behind his paper to snag his mug of coffee. "Hollywood is coming to Rosedale."

"Please pass the sugar," Gina chirped.

"What?" Madison asked, leaning forward.

"Please ... pass ... the sugar."

"Not you." Madison waved her little sister's request away. "What was that, Dad?"

Their dad lowered his paper and peered at Madison over the top of it. His black-rimmed glasses were smeary, his hair mussed up. He'd been called in to do an inventory count at Best Buy and hadn't gotten home until after one in the morning. "Apparently they're going to be shooting some fancy TV show right here in our sleepy town of Rosedale."

"Who?"

He glanced back at the paper. "Well, let's see. It says that it's a new series starring Jessica Ashton and Grant Palmer."

"Here?"

"Yup."

"Wow!"

"Sugar, *pull*eaze," Gina groaned, flopping her head on the table.

Madison looked at her little sister, who obviously had *no* idea what a big deal this was. Poor kid. It must suck to be five and so oblivious to the exciting happenings of the world. Madison slid the sugar bowl over, her mind spinning. Real live TV stars were going to be in their town, walking down their streets, buying gas, shopping for groceries? Unbelievable.

Her mom dashed in, slipping a gold criss-cross earring through her earlobe, her black pumps tucked under her arm.

"Mom," Madison said. "Guess what? A TV company is coming to town! Jessica Ashton and Grant Palmer are going to be here from Hollywood."

"That's nice, dear." Her mom grabbed a banana out of the fruit bowl and poured some coffee into her portable coffee mug. "I'm off to the bank. Have a good day, you all." She dropped a kiss on their dad's rumpled hair, another one on Gina, and swung around the table to give Madison a hug. "Be good." And then, like a whirlwind, she was out the door and gone.

"Well," their dad said, a bemused smile on his face as he flipped to the Classifieds section at the back of the paper and ran his finger down the Help Wanted column. "She sure was impressed."

By the time Madison had dropped Gina off at her kindergarten and gotten to the back of the school where her fifth-grade class lined up, it was clear by the excited hubbub that everyone had heard the news. Joey Rodriguez was swaggering around. "I breakah yorah face," he said, talking out of the side of his mouth like an old-time gangster from the movies.

Madison tossed her softball high in the air and caught it, the ball landing in her worn baseball mitt with a satisfying *smack*. She tossed it up again, pretending she didn't see Joey, hoping he'd try to snatch the ball away from her like he did last week. Then she could chase him all over the playground, Joey dodging this way and that.

The ball thumped into the mitt, stinging the palm of her hand a bit. Joey spun around, caught sight of Madison approaching, and lifted an imaginary machine gun. *"Ackka, ackka, ackka,"* he called out, his arms and shoulders vibrating as if the gun had a powerful kickback. *"Dat* will teach you to mess wid Big Joey."

"Big Joey?" Madison snorted, closing her mitt around the ball and tucking it under her arm with a cocky smile. "Sure, whatever you say, pipsqueak."

Joey opened his mouth to shoot a comeback her way, but the bell rang and everyone ran, pushing and shoving to get in line. Ms. Elliot came out, looking pretty as usual. She was wearing a fuzzy, pumpkin-coloured sweater and brown pants. *Very autumnish looking,* Madison thought as she followed Ms. Elliot and the other students in through the metal door, down the hall, and into their classroom.

Madison loved September, the way the air was starting to get a crisp bite to it. Soon the leaves would change colour, transforming the trees into a brilliant sea of crimson, yellow, orange, and brown. Then wind would rattle the branches, causing the leaves to disengage and start their twirling, leaping descent to the ground.

It was an exhilarating time of year. The earth smelled of wet rain and dirt, and the promise of Halloween was peeking around the corner.

And now TV people were coming to town. Maybe they were here already. Wouldn't that be cool?

Madison had barely settled into her seat when she felt the eraser end of Isabelle's pencil poke her in the back.

"Did you hear the news?" Isabelle asked.

"About the TV show?" Isabelle's best friend, Olivia, added from her seat across the aisle. "They've come to town and my mom says it's our big chance. I've been taking her modelling and tap classes since I was five, and when they see how talented I am, they're going to flip out! Seriously, Madison, you should have listened to me and signed up years ago, because the casting directors are *only* going to be interested in people with showbiz experience."

Madison shrugged. "I've never been much for that kind of thing," she said, pretending she didn't care. But really, she'd always wanted to take Olivia's mom's classes. A lot of girls did, and whenever they talked about it, Madison felt like a bit of an outsider. Her parents couldn't afford the fancy fees.

Joey sauntered past. "Hey, Mad-one," he said, cocking his butt in her direction and letting out a big juicy fart.

"Ewww! Joey, you are so disgusting," Madison

squealed, her hand flying to cover her nose and mouth.

"Gross!" Isabelle laughed, batting at him. She'd had a serious crush on him since second grade.

"Joey Rodriguez," Olivia said, tilting her nose disdainfully in the air. "You have no class."

Joey cackled and plopped into his seat. "My pleasure," he replied, doffing an imaginary hat with a flourish. "Let me know, my ladies, if the smell starts to decline and I shall happily send another your way."

"You are one sick puppy," Madison said, wafting her free hand around to help disperse the stench.

"Good morning, class." Ms. Elliot was standing at the front of the room. A new girl with long blond hair was at her side.

"Good morning, Ms. Elliot," the class answered in unison, all eyes focused on the girl.

She was skinny, sun-kissed. There were slight shadows under her violet eyes, as if she hadn't slept well. Madison had never seen anyone with that colour of eyes before. The girl was wearing faded blue jeans with a hole in the knee and a lilac smock top with barely-there butterflies dancing over it. She had a sparkly dragonfly barrette in her hair.

Was she growing out her bangs too? Madison thought, her hand rising up to tug on her own.

"I'd like you to welcome a new student to our class. She's just moved here from ..." Ms. Elliot bent over slightly. "I'm sorry, where are you from, honey?"

"California," the girl said. Her voice was quiet, subdued. She was really pretty. Seemed shy, though. Didn't look up. *Why hadn't she started school last week like everyone else?* Madison wondered. Maybe her parents got the date wrong. Madison was glad her mom and dad didn't make those kinds of mistakes. That would be embarrassing. Was the new girl embarrassed?

Madison felt Isabelle's eraser poke her in the shoulder again. She glanced over. *"California ..."* Isabelle mimicked softly. *"Oohh ..."*

The new girl's face flushed. Madison wondered if she'd heard.

Olivia tittered and leaned across the aisle. "She looks stuck up," she whispered. Isabelle nodded, smirking. Madison turned back to the front.

"She's moved here from California, and her name is ..." Ms. Elliot glanced down at the paper in her hand. "Alyssa Hawkins. It's always a challenge to move to a new town and change schools, so please do your best to make her feel welcome." Ms. Elliot smiled and Alyssa smiled back, but Madison noticed that although the girl's lips were smiling, her eyes seemed scared. *I'm glad I'm not new,* she thought.

2
recess

When the recess bell rang, instead of going outside with Olivia and Isabelle as she usually did, Madison made her way against the flow of bodies surging for the door to where the new girl was standing uncertainly by her desk.

"Hi," Madison said. "Welcome to Rosedale. I'm Madison Stokes."

"Hello," the girl answered, her face cautious. "I'm Alyssa."

"Yes, I know," Madison said, then wished she hadn't because the girl flushed. "Ms. Elliot ..." She shrugged. "Hey, do you want to play some tetherball?"

"What?"

"Tetherball." Madison's face was starting to feel hot.

"Um ... no thanks."

"Okay, sure, no problem. Just thought I'd ask." Madison kept the smile on her face as she turned to head for the door. Olivia was right, the new girl *was* stuck up.

"I ..." Madison heard the girl say. "I don't know what tetherball is. I mean, maybe I'd like it if I knew how, but it's my first day and ..." Madison turned back. Alyssa had a rueful smile on her face. "I don't want to make a fool of myself in front of everybody."

"Oh!" Madison laughed, a wave of relief washing over her. "I thought I was bothering you or something."

"No way," Alyssa said and laughed too. "Are you kidding me? I was standing here, not sure what to do, knowing I had to go outside but dreading the thought of all those eyes staring at me." She shuddered. "I *hate* being new!"

"You've been new before?"

"Sure, haven't you?"

"I was born here," Madison said, feeling a little embarrassed, like maybe Alyssa would think she was boring. Not only was Madison born in Rosedale, but her mother and father were, too. They'd been high school sweethearts. And her grandma and grandpa had lived in Rosedale all their lives as well. They lived only two blocks away with Sadie, their big calico cat.

"You are so lucky," Alyssa said. "We're always moving. It stinks. Always on the go, living out of suitcases, packing and unpacking, never able to put down roots, join clubs, make friends."

"Wow, I never thought of it like that."

They were quiet for a moment, but it wasn't an uncomfortable silence.

"What do your parents do?" Madison asked. "That you've got to move so much?"

A flash of something—Madison couldn't quite put her finger on it—flickered across Alyssa's face.

"Oh," Alyssa said with a shake of her head, "parents are so boring. Let's talk about something else."

"Sure," Madison said. "Fine by me."

A thunk on the window caused both girls to jump. A sparrow wobbled away from the glass, wings flopping drunkenly for a second or two until it grew steadier and flew off.

"Poor bird," Alyssa said.

"Yeah. I'm glad it's okay."

"Me too. Birds were always flying into the big window we had in our last place. Sometimes they were all right, but sometimes they'd break their necks and Berta and I had to bury them."

"Who's Berta? Your friend?"

"No."

"Sister?"

"Housekeeper." Alyssa's voice was suddenly abrupt.

"A housekeeper?" Madison didn't know anyone who had a housekeeper. She was about to ask more questions, but noticed that Alyssa had that closed, cautious look on her face again. "You want to go outside and walk around?"

"Okay."

They'd made it out of the classroom and halfway down the hall when the bell rang, marking the end of recess. Both girls started laughing.

"So much for walking outside," Alyssa said.

"I'll show you around at lunch if you'd like."

"I would love that." Alyssa smiled, and her whole face seemed to light up. Then the outside doors burst open and the hall filled with a wave of noisy, chattering students headed back to class.

3
compost duty

"And over here," Madison said, leading Alyssa down the hall, "is my bedroom."

"*Our* bedroom," Gina piped up, skipping along behind them. "It's not just yours, half of it belongs to me."

"You share a bedroom?" Alyssa asked.

Madison sighed. "You don't know how lucky you are to be an only child."

"Hey," Gina said, a grin on her face. "I heard that!"

"Gina, get lost," Madison hissed.

"Don't have to," Gina retorted. "It's my room too. You aren't the boss of me."

God, what a pest. They arrived at the bedroom door and Madison reached for the doorknob. "It's a little messy," she said with an apologetic smile. But really, it wasn't. Madison had raced around the night before, cleaning like a madwoman. And not just her side; she'd cleaned Gina's side as well. She'd even gotten up early and made both beds before leaving for school.

Madison swung the door open, stepping back to let her friend enter first.

"Wow," Alyssa chuckled. "I see what you mean."

Madison glanced over Alyssa's shoulder and stopped, horrified. The room was a disaster. There were toys everywhere and the dress-up trunk had been ransacked, its entire contents strewn across the floor. And it wasn't just Gina's side of the room that was messed up. It was clear from the rumpled look of Madison's bedspread that Gina had been jumping on her bed again!

"Why, you little ..." Madison swung around and fixed a look on her sister that should have turned her to stone. But no, Gina just slipped under Madison's arm, darted into the room, and took Alyssa's hand as if Alyssa had come to visit *her*.

"Do you want to play fairy princesses with me?" Gina asked, giving Alyssa her sweetest aren't-I-such-a-cute-little-thing smile.

"Don't you *dare* pull that innocent act with me," Madison said through gritted teeth. "You are *so* dead!"

Gina's eyes widened. She ducked behind Alyssa. "Da*ddy*," Gina screeched at the top of her lungs. "*Daddy!*"

Madison's dad poked his head out of the laundry room. "What's going on?"

Gina darted around Alyssa. Madison lunged, but she was too late: Gina was safely past and tearing down the hall toward their dad. "Madison threatened to *kill* me!" she wailed, flinging her arms around his legs and bursting into noisy crocodile tears.

"Madison Harriet Stokes," her father said, his voice dropping into the you're-in-trouble register.

Alyssa glanced over at her, quirking an eyebrow. "Harriet?" she mouthed.

Madison stifled a groan. "My grandmother's mother."

"Ohhh ..." Alyssa said, smothering a laugh.

Her dad lifted Gina up onto his hip. Gina buried her face into his chest, but not before Madison caught sight of a smug little smile on her tear-streaked face. "Is this true?" their dad said. "Did you threaten your sister?"

Madison's gaze travelled from Gina to her dad's stern look. "Dad, she——"

"That's a yes or no question," he said, cutting her off.

Madison knew the expression on his face very well. "Yes," she said.

"Seriously, you don't have to help." Madison tried to breathe shallowly, holding the stinky compost container as far away from her body as she could.

"I don't mind. Here, let me get that." Stepping in front of Madison, Alyssa unlatched the kitchen's screen door and swung it open. A large black fly that had been bumping against the screen zigzagged in.

Madison walked onto the back porch and started down the steps into the heat of the day. "Thanks."

"What else?" Alyssa asked.

Madison tipped her head toward the weather-beaten shed at the back of the yard. "If you could get the shovel from the shed and bring it around to the front yard, that would be great."

"Okay." Alyssa headed for the shed as Madison walked around to the side of the house. It was cooler in the shade, insects hummed. It would almost be nice if she wasn't on garbage duty. She quickened her step. The sooner she got the contents of this smelly bucket into the ground and composting, the happier she'd be. How embarrassing that she had to do it now, with her new friend in tow. Dad was usually fair and even-tempered, but lately he'd been grouchy about the smallest things. Madison's mom said he was getting frustrated about his work situation, chasing down job leads and nothing panning out. But still, he hadn't even listened to her side of things. Gina complained, pulled out the tears, and Madison got a lecture and was put on compost duty. *Little sisters.* Madison shook her head, disgusted. *They were nothing but trouble.*

By the time Alyssa arrived with the shovel, Madison had already found a good spot by the rose bush against the front fence. She placed the compost bucket to the side and dug a hole, the sun beating down, making her nose sweat. Once the hole was dug, she dumped the compost in. "You might want to back up," she told Alyssa. "This is the smelliest part." But instead Alyssa took turns with the shovel, chopping the food garbage into small pieces so it would compost better. Then they shovelled the dirt back over it and started stomping it down. Madison wasn't sure how it happened, but the next thing she knew, they were pretending to do a rain dance, whooping and hollering, their feet beating time, dust clouds flying up.

"Oh … my god … will you look at that?"

Madison glanced over. Olivia and Isabelle were walking toward them on the sidewalk. They were obviously going for the twins look: same shirt, same designer jeans, their hair French-braided on the sides and swept into a high ponytail. They came to a halt, fancy shopping bags in their hands, and stared at her and Alyssa as if they were lunatics.

Olivia and Isabelle never used to act so superior. But ever since lunch on Alyssa's second day at school—when Isabelle and Olivia had sat with them and peppered Alyssa with a zillion questions—things had turned bad. They'd wanted to know what it was like living in California. And had Alyssa met any movie stars? No? Well, had she ever seen any? Perfectly normal questions. Madison would have asked a few questions about Los Angeles herself, but she could tell it was making Alyssa uncomfortable. She was scrunched down into her hoodie, pushing her food around, her face shut, but Olivia didn't seem to notice.

"Oh," Olivia had said, shaking her head. "You should have taken one of those star tours. They drive you to movie stars' houses. I did that tour last year when my family went to L.A. Not only that, but my mom went online and got us seats to be in the *audience* for the taping of *The Tonight Show*! That was cool. You should have done that!"

"I'm not much of a fan of *The Tonight Show*," Alyssa said, getting up from the table. "How about a game of tetherball?" she asked Madison, and strode off without waiting for an answer.

"Boy, what a snob," Olivia said.

"Yeah, who does she think she is?" Isabelle agreed.

"I think she's just ..." Madison got up from the table. "Shy or something."

"My vote is for 'something,'" Isabelle snorted. And that was that. Ever since then they'd had it in for Alyssa.

Now Isabelle nudged Olivia and laughed, but it wasn't a nice one. "What are they *doing*?" she said, her shopping bags swaying.

Madison straightened slowly. She could feel embarrassed heat flooding her face. "Um ..." she said. "We're ... ah ..."

"Composting," Alyssa piped up, breezy as could be. "Saving the earth. All in a day's work. What are *you* two doing?" Alyssa glanced pointedly at the bags in their hands. "Shopping? Oh my, that's admirable."

Madison bit back a smile. She didn't dare look over at Alyssa, didn't have to: she knew the mischievous expression she'd find on her friend's face. How had she ever thought Alyssa was *shy*?

"Why is she here?" Isabelle asked Madison, waving her fingers in Alyssa's direction. "Who invited her to your house?"

"I did," Madison said. She didn't know why she was feeling on the defensive. It was her yard and she could have whomever she wanted in it.

"But we bought some new clothes and wanted to do a fashion show for you," Olivia said with a pout.

"That's fine," Madison said. "You still can. Alyssa likes fashion shows, don't you, Alyssa?"

Alyssa quirked an eyebrow at her. "Oh sure," she said, unsuccessfully trying to suppress a smirk. "I just love watching other people show off their new clothes." And there was something about the look in Alyssa's eyes that set Madison off. An unexpected hoot of laughter started to rise up. She clamped her lips together, trying to squash it down, but it was too powerful to be denied and erupted out of her nose in a loud, unladylike snort.

Olivia's and Isabelle's heads swivelled in unison to stare at her.

"Sorry," Madison managed to gasp out, keeping her head tucked down so they wouldn't see the merriment on her face. "I think I swallowed a fly ... must get water ..." She ran to the house, doubled over, clutching her stomach, suppressed snort-laughs erupting like miniature volcanoes.

"Are you coming in?" she heard Alyssa ask. Neither Olivia nor Isabelle answered. "All right then," Alyssa said, sauntering off in Madison's wake, cool as ever. "See you later."

Madison managed to stuff the giggles down long enough to turn back and give a wave before she and Alyssa disappeared into her house. The door shut behind them and they collapsed on the kitchen floor, overcome with laughter.

"Are they gone?" Madison asked a little while later, sitting up and wiping the tears from her eyes.

Alyssa peeked out the window. "Coast is clear."

"Oh good, because we have to go out there and roll a couple rocks over what we buried, or else the squirrels will dig up the compost and spread it all over the lawn." And somehow that made the two girls crack up all over again.

4
alyssa's dad

The next day at recess, Madison and Alyssa commandeered the tall swings.

"Since we'll be in middle school next year," Alyssa had remarked in the morning lineup, "this is our last hurrah at childish things, like swings and teeter-totters, and we should make the most of it while we can. Let's not leave elementary school with any regrets."

It was a good idea. Madison hadn't swung in ages. She leaned back, pulling hard, her toes stretching toward the brilliant blue sky and beyond. It almost felt that if she got high enough, she could let go and sail out to dance on the soft, puffy clouds rolling past, and then gently float back down to earth.

"Hey, thanks for having me over yesterday," Alyssa called out.

"Yeah." Madison shook her head ruefully. "Sorry about my dad making us do chores."

"Are you kidding me? It was fun!"

Madison looked over to see if she was joking, but Alyssa didn't appear to be. Her face was tilted up to the sun, her eyes closed as if she were savouring the feeling of the wind rushing past, blond hair streaming behind her like a banner. And then the swing, having reached its peak, reversed and Alyssa's hair blew forward, obscuring her face.

Madison did another hard pump, then launched herself out of the swing and sailed through the air, staggering a bit when she landed with a jolt in the sand. "Really?"

"You bet."

"Hey, maybe next time we can go to your house. That way we won't have to deal with chores or my pesky little sister."

"Mmm ..." said Alyssa. She released her grip on the swing's chains and soared, arms and legs waving as she hurtled through space and landed beside Madison on her butt. "Oof!"

"What do you think?" Madison asked, helping Alyssa to her feet.

"I don't know." Alyssa shrugged as she dusted the sand off the seat of her pants. "I love being at your house. Your dad is such a cutie-pie. Sure, he got grouchy, but then he made fresh lemonade and those Rice Krispie treats for us. Whose dad does that?" A wistful expression crossed Alyssa's face. "You don't know how lucky you are."

"I guess so. What's your dad like?"

"What?" Alyssa said, which was weird, because it's not like she couldn't hear her. They were standing right next to each other.

"Your dad," Madison repeated. "What's he like?" She was just making conversation, but the minute the question was out of her mouth, she wished she could stuff it back in again, because it was clear by Alyssa's expression that it wasn't a good subject.

The bell rang. "Recess is over," Alyssa said, turning and running toward the school. Madison followed, momentarily relieved.

But once she was back at her desk, with Ms. Elliot up at the front talking about the structural components of atoms, her thoughts turned back to Alyssa and the look on her face when Madison had asked about her dad.

5
questions

"What are you thinking about, sweetheart?"

"Huh?" Madison glanced over at her mom on the sofa beside her.

"You've been staring at that same page for the last five minutes," her mother said, putting the last stitch in, then looping her needle over and around the thread to make a knot. "Not to mention the slight scowl on your face." She snipped the thread and handed Gina her much-mended stuffed bunny with the floppy ears.

"Thanks, Mommy," Gina said. She gave her stuffed animal a kiss and a hug and then danced it down the hall to their bedroom.

"I'm not scowling," Madison said, but she was. She could feel the tension in her forehead where it had been scrunched together.

"I stand corrected," Madison's mother said, her face solemn, but there was no mistaking the twinkling in her eyes. She took one of Madison's dad's navy work shirts out of her mending basket. One of the buttons was missing. Her mother rummaged around in her button stash and found one that would work.

"Mom?"

"Yes, honey?"

"Why do you think Alyssa has never had me over? In the last two weeks, she's come here three times, but whenever I mention going to her place, she changes the subject. Maybe she doesn't really like me, and just says yes because she's new and doesn't have any friends and doesn't want to hurt my feelings?"

"Well," Madison's mother began, her needle sliding in and out of the holes in the button, trailing dark blue thread. "If you want an unbiased opinion, I'd say she's really happy you met. When she comes over here, you both seem to be having fun. There's a lot of laughter and conversation and—"

"Mom," Madison broke in. "You aren't unbiased. I'm your daughter. Of *course* you're going to think she likes me."

"I don't *think*, honey. I *know*."

"But Mom, she's been to our house *three*

times and I've never been to hers. I don't even know where she lives."

"Maybe she's embarrassed about her home?"

"Why would she be embarrassed about her home?"

"Who knows? Maybe her parents haven't been as blessed as we've been. Your father and I are fortunate to have jobs that bring in a steady income. Maybe her parents got laid off and haven't been able to find something new. Look how hard your dad is searching for another part-time job and he's still coming up empty-handed."

"You're right. It could be that. When I asked her about her dad last week, she got a funny look on her face."

"Funny how?"

"Like she was sad. I thought maybe her parents were divorced or he'd died or something, but maybe he just lost his job and is super grouchy and so she doesn't want to bring people home."

"Could be, or maybe the place she lives in is small or messy. If that's the case, then maybe she'd feel shy about inviting you over."

"But if it was a money thing, why would they have a housekeeper?"

"A housekeeper?" Madison's mother's eyebrows rocketed up to her hairline. She blinked once, twice, and then her eyebrows settled back into their normal place. "Well, perhaps it's something else. Maybe a relative who needs extra care is staying with them, or maybe one of her parents has medical issues and would find it difficult to cope with extra bodies running around."

"Maybe," Madison said, snuggling into her mother's side. She was glad her mom wasn't having medical issues.

"Be careful of the needle, love bug," her mother said, dropping a kiss on the top of Madison's head. They sat in comfortable silence for a while, her mother's shoulder shifting slightly as her hand dipped to and fro. It was as if the shirt was a pond and the needle was a bird dipping its beak to take a drink. "Why don't you talk with her about it? That way, the question won't be sitting like a huge lump between the two of you."

"Yeah, maybe I will." As the words came out of Madison's mouth, she got a nervous thrumming in her belly, but she wasn't going to let that stop her. She was determined to be brave. Tomorrow, when Alyssa came over after school, she would broach the subject.

6
cooking

"I've chopped the pecans. What's next?" Alyssa asked, her eyes glowing. She was wearing Madison's mother's pink apron that had the cowgirls with red lipstick and lassos frolicking all over it. Madison had her dad's "Kiss the Cook" apron on. It was black and way too big. She'd had to wrap the strings around her waist three times before she could tie them. It smelled of her dad and smoke and BBQ sauce.

Madison checked the recipe. "Okay, now we stir in the chocolate chips and the pecans, then we plop rounded tablespoons of the cookie dough onto ungreased cookie sheets and bake at 375 degrees. Do you want to sprinkle the stuff in or stir?"

"Stir." Alyssa grabbed the spoon and started mashing the dough with gusto as Madison slid the pecans off the chopping board into the metal bowl. Then she measured two cups of chocolate chips and put those in as well. "This is the life!" Alyssa exclaimed as she snagged a couple of chocolate chips and popped them in her mouth. "You are *so* lucky."

"Yeah." Madison rolled a few chips around on her tongue, letting their chocolatey goodness melt in her mouth. It was funny how much Alyssa liked to do ordinary things like this.

They dropped rounded mounds of cookie dough on the cookie sheets, the dough sticky on their fingers. Then, when the sheet was full, they slid it into the hot oven carefully, shut the oven door, and set the timer for ten minutes.

"Now what?" Alyssa asked, turning to Madison with a smile.

"I guess we'll straighten up, so Mom doesn't have a conniption fit when she gets home from work."

"A *conniption* fit?" Alyssa giggled.

"What?" Madison asked. "What's so funny?"

"You and your fancy words."

"*Conniption* is not fancy," Madison said, but that just made Alyssa's grin bigger.

"And I suppose you know what it means, too?"

Conniption: a fit of hysteria, rage. Madison

shrugged. "Yeah," she admitted. "I guess I inherited my obsession with words from my grandpa. He's a dictionary, Scrabble tile—laying freak."

"I think it's great you're so close to your grandpa." Alyssa turned to the counter. "All right, let's clean up this mess before your mom has a *conniption* fit." She said the new word carefully, then smiled as if it had felt good banging around in her mouth. "I'll do the dishes and you can put the ingredients away since you know where they go." Alyssa gathered up the measuring cup, the measuring spoons, and the bowl they'd used and headed over to the sink.

Madison knew it probably wasn't the best timing, but figured if she waited for the perfect moment, she might never get her courage up. "Lyssa?" she said, her face suddenly hot. "I was wondering ... um ... if sometime maybe we could go over to your house."

Alyssa's hand was just about to turn on the water. It paused. Her back was to Madison so she couldn't see her face, but Madison could feel the sudden tension that was ricocheting off her body. "Why?" Alyssa asked. Her voice sounded funny.

"Or not. We don't have to. I just thought ..." Madison was going to leave it at that, but a voice inside said, *This is stupid. Just say what you mean.*

She took a deep breath. "It's just that you've been over to my house a bunch of times, but I've never been to yours. I was worried that maybe it was because you didn't really like me. But my mom said she was certain that you did and that maybe a family member was sick or your house was a little messy or something and I told her it couldn't be that because ..." She trailed off, embarrassed.

"You thought I didn't like you?"

"Well, yeah. It crossed my mind."

"Are you kidding me?" Alyssa turned from the sink, the look on her face intense. "I *love* coming over here. It's so different from my house, so normal and homey. Really, seriously, you have *no* idea how lucky you are! I *hate* the way we live." Bright rosy splotches stained her cheeks. "Our home is the complete opposite of this. I've never asked you to come over because I figured you wouldn't want to come. Wouldn't have any fun. With everything having to be so correct and in its place—"

"I don't care what your house is like," Madison said, cutting her off. "Wherever we go, we'll have a good time. It doesn't matter to me if your place is small or if you have a sick grandma sleeping on the sofa. I can help you make her tea, or whatever. That's what friends do. They go over to each other's houses, they share lives and secrets and good times as well as bad." It surprised Madison that her eyes were moist. She hadn't realized quite how scary and important this was to her until she said it out loud. It wasn't like she didn't have other friends and go to their houses. She'd been to Olivia's house, and Isabelle's, too. So why did this feel different? *Because Alyssa's not boring,* a voice said in her head, and it was true. Madison had gone over to other people's homes and they came to hers. They did the things girls her age were supposed to enjoy and Madison would pretend she was interested too, when really, she was bored to death.

It wasn't like that with Alyssa. It was fun, easy, and lately Madison had been getting a hopeful feeling that perhaps someday they'd be best friends. She swallowed hard. Had she ruined it now?

There was the sound of the front door opening. "I'm home," Madison's mother called.

"Mommy!" Gina's muffled voice bellowed from their bedroom. Madison heard their bedroom door thump against the wall and Gina's footsteps thundering down the hall.

The air in the kitchen was thick with words spoken and unspoken. Alyssa looked down at the dirty mixing bowl in her hands as if she was surprised to see that it was still there.

"Okay," Alyssa said, shaking her head as though she thought it was a big mistake. "If you're sure you want to ..."

"I would love to," Madison said, jumping in before Alyssa changed her mind, a light, happy feeling surging through her. "I would absolutely love to."

"All right," Alyssa said and sighed. "But I'm warning you, you aren't going to like it."

7
maximilian

Madison was on pins and needles, trying not to fixate on the large clock that rested above the brightly decorated bulletin board with its colourful autumn leaves and some of her class-mates' compositions about the month of October. She was glad she was in Ms. Elliot's class. The other fifth-grade class had Mrs. Hanson, who was very old and rarely smiled. Mrs. Hanson was all business. There were no gaily decorated bulletin boards in *her* classroom.

Madison's gaze drifted down the bulletin board to the paper she'd written about crisp apples, leaves crunching underfoot, and Halloween, of course. In the top right-hand corner, she'd drawn a witch on a broomstick hovering over her name. Ms. Elliot had written a scrawling A+ in red ink on it.

She glanced up at the clock again: three more minutes to go. Madison sighed and looked back at the worksheet on her desk. Division. Yuck!

It felt like the school day would never end. Every tick of the second hand seemed to take forever. Ms. Elliot had spoken twice to her about fidgeting, but really, it wasn't her fault. Today was the day she was finally going to Alyssa's house.

"I hope her family likes me," Madison had said last night at the dinner table, twisting her napkin in her hands, her appetite gone.

"I'm sure they will," her mother replied.

"What's not to like?" Her dad smiled and reached over, tousling her hair.

"*I* like you!" Gina chimed in, her feet swinging happily.

Madison looked at the supportive faces of her family. *Lyssa's right, I am lucky,* she thought.

"I wonder what her parents do?" her mom asked, spearing another slice of meatloaf and putting it on her plate.

"I have no idea," Madison said. It was odd that she didn't know anything about Alyssa's family. Whenever the subject of Alyssa's home life came up, they somehow got sidetracked onto a new subject.

"Whatever it is, it must be interesting," her

dad said. "And high-powered too, if they have to keep packing up for work." He looked a little wistful. "Must be on the fast track, career-wise."

"Aw, Robert," said Madison's mom, patting his hand. "We like you just the way you are." And he smiled kind of shyly, but looked relieved and pleased too.

The dismissal bell sounded, jolting Madison out of her thoughts. She slipped the half-finished worksheet into her desk and jumped up from her seat. Then she smiled over at Alyssa, but Alyssa didn't smile back. The girls got their stuff from the cubbies and walked out of the classroom.

The hall was a crowded, noisy jostle of kids surging for the exit doors. "Use your walking feet," Madison heard Mrs. Wadsworth call to her fourth-grade class through the doorway. Madison glanced in. Mrs. Wadsworth looked flushed and tired. She was pregnant. It was hard to imagine that a baby was going to come out of that enormous belly of hers. Wisps of hair had escaped from the clasp she wore to tie it back. A few of her students slowed slightly, but the minute they were out of her sight, the speed-walk turned into a run again.

A paper airplane swooping overhead did a loop-the-loop before landing gracefully in a grey garbage can. She heard a familiar "Whoohoo!"

and glanced over to see Joey high-fiving Dylan
Shumack.

The two girls stepped outside. There was a
chill in the afternoon air that Madison found
invigorating. The sun was feebly making its way
through a gap in a bank of fast-moving clouds.
Down the steps the girls went and across the
schoolyard. When they got to the sidewalk,
Alyssa turned left. She was walking fast, her
hoodie pulled up, covering her head. Madison
loved that hoodie. The colour reminded her of
the hyacinths that bloomed outside the living
room window of her grandma and grandpa's
house. She wished she had a hoodie that colour,
but they didn't sell fancy colours like that in
Rosedale.

"I'm really excited to be going over to your
house for dinner," Madison said. "My dad's not
working today. He said I can give him a call when
we're done and he'll pick me up."

Alyssa grunted. She wasn't in a talking mood.

"Is it a long walk?"

Alyssa shook her head, picking up the pace
a bit.

Madison got a dropping feeling in her
stomach. Maybe this was a mistake. She shouldn't
have suggested coming over. She should have let
things be. "I was really glad when the bell rang."

Her voice came out sounding too high-pitched and shiny, but she couldn't seem to keep her nervous chatter inside. "Math makes my brain hurt." She laughed.

Alyssa stopped suddenly.

"Oof," Madison gasped as she crashed into her. "Sorry about that. Are you okay?"

"My shoe," Alyssa said, bending over and untying the lace. "It was coming undone." But it wasn't. She started retying it slowly.

Olivia and Isabelle were coming up behind them on the sidewalk. "My mom has done some sleuthing and she says they're supposed to be shooting sometime this week in the old Gossling cemetery." Olivia was pretending to talk only to Isabelle, but her voice was way louder than necessary. "So we're supposed to go straight home and then she's going to throw my hair into some curlers for five minutes, comb it out, and take us over there. I'll just die if I don't get discovered soon."

"Oh darn," Alyssa muttered. "I can't get this lace right." She untied it again.

"Hi, Madison," the girls said as they passed.

"Hey," Madison replied.

Alyssa stayed in her kneeling position, her fingers holding her perfectly tied shoelace, watching intently until Olivia and Isabelle turned the corner. Then her head flipped around to scan the street in the other direction. "Come on," she whispered, her voice hoarse.

The next thing Madison knew, Alyssa had yanked her into an alley, which was weird because Madison had walked along this block a million times and never noticed it before.

The air was even cooler in the alley, and kind of gloomy. Except for a couple patches of sunlight, the alley was submerged in dark shadowy shapes. Thick trees overhung the tall wooden fence on one side and the dirty brick wall on the other. Garbage cans lined the fence, stuffed full and smelly. A skinny black-and-white cat was rummaging through one of the cans. It saw them and jumped, as if expecting to be hit, and then ran across their path, disappearing into the shadows.

"What are we doing in here?" Madison asked, her sense of unease growing.

Alyssa didn't answer. She just stalked forward, her jaw set.

As Madison's eyes adjusted to the gloom, she noticed that the alley was a dead end, and that a little way down, a glossy black town car was parked with its engine running. *Why doesn't that guy turn off his car?* was her first thought, because everyone knew that leaving an engine running was bad for the environment. *Guy?* was her second, because even though the car had a dark-tinted windshield, Madison could make out the shape of a huge, hulking mammoth sitting behind the steering wheel.

"Uh ... Lyssa ..." All the moisture in Madison's mouth had vanished. "This doesn't appear to be a through road. I think maybe we should turn back." Alyssa didn't seem to hear, and kept marching resolutely forward.

Madison grabbed her arm. "Seriously, Lyssa, I think we should turn back."

Alyssa whirled to face her. "Do you want to come to my house or not?"

Madison nodded.

"Then come on," Alyssa said, striding toward the car.

The car door opened and a gargantuan guy got out. He was wearing a black suit and tie, a white collared shirt, and mirrored sunglasses. His hair was cropped short, army style. He smiled, and a diamond embedded in his front tooth flashed. Madison didn't think a smile could make someone seem even more menacing, but it did. He took a few steps forward.

"Lyssa ..." Madison squeaked as she tried to get her legs to unroot from the ground. "Run," she croaked. But the guy didn't grab her. Instead he walked around the front of the car and opened the back door.

"Max," Alyssa said, giving him a curt nod and then sliding into the back seat.

"Miss?" The guy's head swivelled around to fixate on Madison. A too-perfect eyebrow lifted over the steel-grey frames of his sunglasses. *Does he pluck them?* Madison wondered. Which was a weird thing to think. Why would a guy groom his eyebrows? A girl maybe ... but a man?

"Are you coming or what?" Alyssa's voice jolted Madison into motion. She walked gingerly around the giant, giving herself plenty of room to leap out of the way in case he tried to grab her. She got to where she could see Alyssa.

"Do you know this guy?" she whispered.

Alyssa rolled her eyes. "Of course I know him. Do you really think I'd be stupid enough to get in the car if I didn't? Sheesh!"

"Maximilian at your service," the man said with a sort of German-sounding accent. He gestured with his hand for her to get in. Madison had the sense that he was laughing at her, even though not a flicker of emotion had crossed his face.

She got into the car. It was super clean. Everything was polished and buffed, from the wood inlay and shiny chrome to the leather seats.

Bottles of chilled Evian water rested in the drink holders. "Wow," she whispered.

"Whatever," Alyssa said, turning her head to look out the window.

"Is he your father?" Madison said, still in a whisper.

"No."

"Oh."

Maximilian crossed back around the front of the car.

"Is he from Germany?"

"Austria."

"Oh."

He got in the car. "How vas school?" he asked. It sounded funny to hear such a commonplace question come out of Terminator-man's mouth.

"It sucked," Alyssa said with a scowl, her arms slammed shut across her chest.

"Okey-doke," Maximilian said.

After that, no one spoke. They drove the rest of the way in silence.

8
alyssa's house

Madison had lived in Rosedale all her life. Sure, she'd gone to Willows Beach at the edge of town, just like everyone else on hot summer days. She'd stretched out on her blue-and-white striped beach towel, warm and toasty on the hot pebbles, a welcome relief after braving the frigid, breath-stealing ocean water. Even in the summer, that water was cold. Later she'd make her way to the snack shack, Gina's sticky fingers tucked in one hand, money in the other for ice cream or greasy homemade french fries slathered with ketchup. But Willows Beach was as far north as her family had ever ventured. She'd always figured that after the beach, it was just shrubs and trees and then endless road leading to other towns and cities and places far away. She had no idea that past the beach, and

still officially in Rosedale, there were homes this fancy. Mansions. That's what they were.

The car turned right onto a wide driveway. There was a high granite wall surrounding the property. Maximilian slipped a remote control from his jacket pocket and pointed it at the massive wooden gate with black iron hinges, causing it to slowly, soundlessly swing inward. Once the gate was open, he drove the car through, then waited until the gate closed behind them before driving on.

Madison turned to Alyssa. She knew her eyes must be the size of saucers, but she couldn't help it. "Is *this* your home?" she squeaked.

"No," Alyssa replied. She looked embarrassed, as if it was a bad thing to have a fancy driveway and a magic opening gate like that. "We're just renting. It's only temporary. Has nothing to do with us."

"Still," Madison said. She would have said more, but the car rounded a curve in the driveway—and there before them was the hugest house Madison had ever seen. "Holy cow," she breathed.

The car glided to a stop. Maximilian got out, rounded the car, and opened the back door. Madison slid along the seat and followed Alyssa out. "Thank you," she said to Maximilian, who

was standing at attention by the door. She had to look *way* up. He nodded his head and smiled at her. She tried not to stare at the diamond. Madison wondered if it scraped against his lip. She wanted to ask him, but instead she followed Alyssa up the front steps, feeling awkward, all fingers and thumbs.

Alyssa rang the doorbell, which seemed weird. Who rings the doorbell at their own house? All the kids she knew had a key in their pocket or around their neck on a shoelace or something.

"*Un momentito,*" someone inside called. A second later the door swung open and there was a smiling, plump, middle-aged woman with a halo of frizzy black hair streaked with silver. She was wearing a sturdy black dress and a white apron tied at the back. "*Hola!*" she said. "*Tuviste un buen día en la escuela?*"

"*Tan tan,*" Alyssa said, shrugging as they stepped into a big, gleaming foyer. "*Este es mi amiga, Madison.*"

Madison's jaw dropped. "You ... you can speak Spanish?" she stammered.

Alyssa shrugged again, like it was no big deal.

"Wow. Incredible."

"Madison," Alyssa said, gesturing toward the woman, "this is our housekeeper, Berta."

"Estoy contento encontrarle," Berta said, smiling and nodding.

"Huh?"

"She said she's pleased to meet you," Alyssa said.

"Oh." Madison flushed. "Nice to meet you too."

"Quieres una merienda?" Berta asked. *"Tal vez un poco de jugo?"*

"Um ..."

"She wants to know if you'd like something to eat or juice or something," Alyssa explained, looking bored.

"Uh ... okay ..." Madison felt gawky, like a country bumpkin. "Juice would be fine."

As far as Madison could see, the house and its furnishings were white: soaring white walls, curving white archways, gleaming white marble floors with tiny black-triangle accents. In the vast room beyond the foyer were white sofas, sheer white curtains, and a large glass vase on a clear glass table filled with perfect long-stemmed white lilies whose thick, waxy green leaves bowed gracefully outward. Beyond that, through the enormous windows that practically covered an entire wall, was an expansive green lawn dotted with massive red cedar trees. At the edge of the lawn was a pristine beach with sparkling blue-green water that extended to the horizon.

A perfect little white sailboat bobbed on the ocean, listing to one side, catching the wind. And it looked so right that for a second Madison wondered if Lyssa's family paid the sailor to stay in that spot. The idea of it made a smile dance on her lips. Luckily, Alyssa had already turned back to the housekeeper.

"*Sí. Muchas gracias, Berta,*" Alyssa said. "*Vamos a estar en mi habitacion.*"

Berta nodded and disappeared down a long marble hallway. The house was quiet now, everything still. Madison could hear a clock ticking from somewhere in the living room. "I suppose you want to see my bedroom?" Alyssa's face and tone were flat, as if she couldn't care less if Madison said yes or no.

Madison took a breath, trying to centre herself. She didn't know why Lyssa was acting so cold, angry almost, but she had the feeling that she needed to tread carefully or the whole friendship could blow over like a house of cards. "Sure," she said.

She followed her friend up a wide staircase to the second floor. Everything was perfect there as well. It looked like a magazine. Not a single speck of dust.

"Here it is," Alyssa said, opening a door and stepping inside. "My so-called room." She looked around with a weird expression on her face, as if the room had a bad odour that only she could smell. "I hate it," she said, her voice suddenly so low that Madison almost didn't hear her, but she did. And the suppressed vehemence in it made Madison need to look away.

She glanced around the room, keeping her face neutral. It was a good size and had a gorgeous view of the ocean. There was a fancy white bedspread with enough pillows stacked up against the headboard to drown in, topped off with a little pale yellow throw pillow that had a curly-haired cherub embroidered on the front. A modern, glossy black desk stood in the corner with a vase of pale yellow roses, and a lamp and an armchair were positioned by the fireplace, but again, not a thing was out of place. "Yeah, I see what you mean. It's pretty and all, but it doesn't feel like you. Feels sort of like a grownup's room or something. Where's your stuff? Where's the mess?"

Alyssa snorted. "Yeah, that would be the day. Everything," she mimicked, "*must* be in its place."

"Why?"

"I don't know. It's always been this way." She was standing in the middle of her room now, as if she were a visitor. "My mom's got a thing about keeping things tidy. It's like if things don't *look* perfect all the time, then maybe that means things *aren't* perfect. And I try. I really try. I don't want to disappoint her, but have you ever tried being perfect?" Alyssa suddenly looked weary and sort of lost. "It's …" She breathed in, her breath shaky. "It's an impossible task." And to the surprise of them both, Alyssa started to weep.

9

art

There was a soft knock. *"Tu merienda esta lista,"* Berta called through the door.

"Bien gracias," Alyssa replied, her voice sounding totally normal. *"Vamos a la derecha abajo."*

"Wow," Madison said, trying to lighten the mood, after the soft shuffle of Berta's feet had disappeared down the hall. "You're good! You should try to get a job on that TV thing they're making. Seriously, I never would have guessed you'd just been crying."

"Blech!" Alyssa made a face. "I'd never in a million years want to be an actress."

"Why not?"

Alyssa walked over to her bedside table, got a Kleenex, and blew her nose. "I think it would suck, everyone looking at you all the time, following you around, watching and gossiping about you. I would *never* choose that for my life!"

"Oh, I don't know," Madison said, shaking her head. "Think about all the glamour and the money and the fame, everyone knowing your name, wanting to be around you, jet-setting around the world."

Alyssa swiped another Kleenex across her wet eyes and tossed it into the wastebasket by the night table. "I imagine the whole thing is highly overrated." She squared her shoulders. "Anyway, enough of that. Ready for a snack?"

She led the way down to the living room, where Berta had laid out a plate with thin cucumber slices and carrot and celery sticks surrounding a little bowl with some sort of dip.

Madison was a bit nervous about trying it, but she didn't want to be rude, so she copied Alyssa and dipped her carrot stick in. It tasted good. "What is this stuff?"

"Hummus. It's a kind of bean dip, healthy of course. You don't have to eat it if you don't want to."

"No, I like it."

Alyssa tipped her head and looked at Madison as if trying to see past the skin to the truth underneath. "Okay," she said finally, her shoulders relaxing slightly. "Me too."

After their snack they played on the beach, threw rocks in the water and watched them splash, then searched for the prettiest pebbles to tuck into their pockets.

"Let's run," Madison said, and so they did. They ran down the beach for no reason other than it was fun. It felt different from running on concrete or grass—harder, more awkward, their feet sinking in, skidding, slipping slightly on the combination of pebbles and grit. Pushing their way forward, they were buffeted by the wind off the ocean tossing their hair up into the air, swirling it around their faces, the faint taste of salt on their lips.

They came to the end, where the sloping shore gave way to dark jutting rocks rising upward to form a cliff wall. Seagulls circled above, their cries a shrill punctuation mingling with the sound of the surf. The girls stopped running and bent over, hands on their knees, breathing hard.

Alyssa was the first to straighten. She looked out over the ocean. "Do you want to see my art studio? It's in the boathouse." She said it nonchalantly, like it was no big deal, but Madison could tell that it was.

"I'd love to," Madison said. Alyssa's shoulders seemed to relax, as though she'd let out a breath she'd been holding.

When they arrived at the boathouse, Alyssa paused, her hand on the doorknob. "Don't tell anyone at school, okay?"

"Course not," Madison said.

"Thanks." Alyssa turned the knob. "My art's private. I don't show it to many people." She swung the door open and Madison followed her inside.

She was immediately struck by how different the boathouse felt from the fancy house Alyssa lived in. It smelled of oil paints and turpentine. An old wooden picnic table in the centre of the room was covered with jars of brushes, crumpled paper, paint rags, and tubes of paint. A partially finished painting leaned on an easel. But the thing that really stopped Madison in her tracks and stole her breath away was the finished painting that was propped against the wall. It was so beautiful, so full of colour and life and passion. It wasn't like anything Madison had ever seen before. "This is *yours?*" she said when she finally found her voice. "You *painted* this?" She turned to Alyssa.

Alyssa nodded. "Yeah. I've got more in storage ..."

"Oh my god ... You are *so* talented! I had no idea."

Alyssa looked down at her hands. "I ... I like to paint. I don't know, it fills me somehow. We move a lot and it's tough; I get lonely, but at least I have my paints. You know?"

"No, I don't. I don't know what it would be like to be able to paint like that. If I had a tenth of your talent, I'd be walking around with my chest puffed up, so proud."

Alyssa laughed, her face shy, and shook her head. "No, I ..."

Madison grabbed her by the shoulders. "Seriously, Alyssa, you *are* an artist!"

"Oh ..." Alyssa's shy smile came out like a ray of sunshine. "I'm glad you like my painting."

"Like it?" Madison gazed around her in awe. "I *love* it!"

10
a different kind of dinner

It was such a different feeling sitting in the dining room after being outside and in Alyssa's studio. It felt stiff and unnatural, just the two of them at the big glossy black table with its silverware, white linen napkins, and heavy crystal water glasses. Madison was a bit nervous. What if she made a mess? The table was so shiny that every spot and splash would show. She glanced down. Good grief. *Three* forks! What were they all for? How was she supposed to know which one to use? "Where's your mom and dad?" Madison asked.

"I don't have a dad."

"How can you not have a——"

"——And my mom's at work," Alyssa said, cutting her off.

Berta came through the swinging kitchen

door and set down a small plate in front of each of them.

"What is this?" Madison whispered to Alyssa.

"Grapefruit and artichoke salad with shaved Parmesan and a honey-lemon dressing."

"Oh." Berta disappeared back into the kitchen. "Everyone has a dad," Madison said. "So your parents are divorced. Big deal. A lot of kids' parents are."

"No," Alyssa said, picking up the fork that was farthest away from her plate. "They aren't divorced. They were never married. I don't even know who he is."

Madison was silent for a moment, taking this in. "How can you not know who he is? Everyone knows who their dad is."

"Well, I don't." Alyssa stabbed a piece of salad.

"Why don't you ask your mom?"

"I have. She doesn't want to discuss it."

"But surely—"

"Can you drop it, please?" Alyssa said, her voice sharp.

"Okay." Madison glanced at Alyssa's place setting, picked up the same fork she had, and poked at the salad. She'd never seen a salad that looked like this before. She speared a piece on her fork and tasted it. It was good.

When they had finished, Berta returned

and whisked their empty plates away. Then she brought the main course: grilled halibut, zucchini, and some cooked grain with diced tomato and onions on top. "It's quinoa," Alyssa said with a grimace. "An ancient grain from back when the pyramids were built."

"Oh." Madison took a polite mouthful.

"It's *very* healthful," Alyssa continued, extending her pinky and putting on a posh lady face. And with that, the awkwardness was broken; both girls started to giggle, the sound bouncing off the walls of the stark room. "And tastes ..." Alyssa smacked her lips delicately together. "Like ... hmmm ... dirty socks?"

"Pfftt," Madison snorted. Unfortunately, a few particles of quinoa escaped from between her compressed lips and landed on the table.

Madison felt her face flush. She tried to mop up the offending particles with her napkin. Her gaze darted to Alyssa, hoping she hadn't noticed, but Alyssa leaned toward her with a smirk. "I saw that," she whispered in a low, fancy-lady voice.

Madison felt her face get even hotter.

"It's no big deal, dear," Alyssa continued, delicately lifting a forkful to her lips, "all the best families do it." She closed her mouth around the quinoa, lowered the fork, tipped her nose in the air, quirked her little pinky, and *pfftt,* sprayed the table in front of her with little grains.

"Alyssa!" Madison gasped, shock and amusement all mixed up.

"Yes?" Alyssa inquired, one eyebrow cocked, staring down the length of her nose like a dowager duchess.

Berta came through the swinging door with a crystal water pitcher, ice cubes clinking, and topped up their water glasses. *"Está todo bien?"*

"Sí," Alyssa replied, suddenly back to normal, her eyes twinkling. *"Todo está bien."*

Berta left again and the girls ate in companionable silence. Madison kept thinking that at any moment, Alyssa's mother would arrive home from work, bustle in with a cheery hello.

Dessert—fresh slices of ripe pineapple—came and went, and still no mom.

After the dessert plates were whisked away, it was time to go home.

Madison was going to phone her dad, but Alyssa called on the intercom for Maximilian, who lived in the gatehouse, and in a couple of minutes the town car came purring down the drive.

"See you tomorrow at school," Alyssa said as the two girls carefully placed her painting in the trunk. Back in the boathouse she had insisted that Madison take the painting as a gift, and Madison, thrilled and embarrassed, had finally accepted.

Madison walked around to where Maximilian was holding the back door open, and slipped into the seat. "Thank you so much. I had a wonderful time and I love, love, love the painting!"

Alyssa smiled and gave a little wave as Maximilian shut the door. Madison turned in her seat, and she watched through the rear window as the car pulled away, Alyssa getting smaller and smaller until finally she disappeared from view.

Madison didn't like leaving her there in that big house with only staff to keep her company, but if she stayed any later, her mom and dad would get worried.

Her dad was in the living room watching TV when she arrived home. "Hey," he said, rising to his feet, "I was going to pick you up." He switched off the TV and gave her a hug. "What do you have there?"

Madison turned the painting around so he could see. "Alyssa gave it to me. She painted it."

He whistled low through his teeth. "Wow." He bent over to look at it more closely. "That girl's got some talent."

"I know," Madison said, feeling proud for her

friend, and wishing Alyssa was there so she could see the admiration on her dad's face.

He straightened, giving his head a shake as if to clear it. "Where do you want to hang it?"

Madison thought for a second, and then it came to her. "I'd like to hang it by my bed, so I can see it as I go to sleep."

"Perfect spot," her dad said. "You put a little X on the wall where you'd like it, and I'll hang the painting tomorrow while you're at school."

"Thanks, Dad," she said, giving him a hug.

Madison headed down the hall. "How was your visit?" she heard her mom call. She paused, glancing in her parents' bedroom . Her mom was stretched out reading a romance novel.

"Oh, fine," Madison replied, continuing on her way, because what was she supposed to say? She didn't want to tell her mom about Lyssa crying and how lonely the house was. She didn't know why. She usually told her mom everything, but somehow this seemed private, like telling someone else would be betraying Alyssa. Maybe tomorrow she would feel differently.

Madison tiptoed into her darkened bedroom, a pale blue glow coming from the seashell nightlight in the corner. Gina, whose bedtime was seven-thirty, was already asleep. Madison propped the painting against her leg as she got a pencil out of her backpack and stuck it between her teeth. Then she picked up the painting and climbed on her bed. Moonlight streaming through the window gave her enough light to see. She held the painting in various spots until she found the perfect one and drew an *X* where the nail should go. She got off the bed, carefully leaned the painting against the wall, then got into her pyjamas, brushed her teeth, washed her face, and tucked into bed.

Madison listened to Gina making snuffling sleep noises. It always ticked her off that she had to share a room with her little sister.

Tonight though, gazing around the room at the jumble of toys, old and new, smiling back at her, she felt good. There were books on the shelf as well as a few lying on the rag rug, stuffed animals overflowing from the chest at the foot of her bed, her troll collection from second grade with their tufts of multicoloured hair marching cheerfully across the windowsill, her faithful baseball bat and mitt propped up in the corner.

She glanced over at Gina's side of the room, and instead of getting grouchy that it looked like a bomb had gone off, Madison found she was smiling. This was how a kid's bedroom should look, cozy and lived in and full of memories.

Alyssa's huge bedroom flashed before her.

Madison snuggled deeper into her comforter. Poor Alyssa. Her room looked like it had been ripped out of the pages of a fancy magazine: pretty, but sort of empty and cold.

I wouldn't want, Madison thought just before she drifted off to sleep, *a bedroom like that.*

the tv people

Madison was standing and pedalling fast, Alyssa behind her on the bike seat, her arms clasped tight around Madison's waist and her legs splayed out to the sides like a circus clown. "This is a blast!" Alyssa yelled over the rushing wind. Madison could tell by her voice that she had a huge grin on her face.

"It sure is." Madison pushed down hard on the pedals. "And it's only the beginning—we've got all of tonight and tomorrow morning, too."

"Heaven ..." Alyssa sang. *"I'm in heaven ..."*

Madison smiled, thinking back to her dad a few months ago, after the call came from Best Buy saying he'd gotten the job. He'd hung up the phone, swept her mom into his arms, and danced her around the living room, singing that very song. Both of them were so happy. He'd been hoping for full-time, but as her parents said, even part-time was a blessing.

Madison took a big breath. *"And my heart beats so that I can hardly speak …"* she sang.

"And I seem to find the happiness I seek," they bellowed together. It was a good feeling. Singing right out loud, not caring who heard or saw them. *"When we're out together dancing cheek to cheek!"*

Alyssa started laughing. "I can't believe you know that old Fred Astaire song!"

Madison shrugged like it was no big deal, but she was proud too. "Yeah, my dad sings that song sometimes." She was glad that Alyssa hadn't gone on to the second verse, since she wasn't sure of the words and it was hard to sing and pedal two people at the same time. She was perspiring, her thighs feeling the burn, everything requiring more effort with two of them on her bike. Only half a block to go, a right on Brighton Avenue, then one more block and they'd be at Shop & Save. "I'm so glad your mom finally said you could sleep over."

"Me too," Alyssa said.

"And I can't believe it's your very first sleep-over *ever!*"

"Yeah … well, we moved a lot and … she's kind of overprotective."

"I'll say." Madison stuck her arm out and bent it at the elbow. It was difficult to do a proper arm signal with the extra weight on the bike. It wobbled rather precariously, but she managed to keep them out of the ditch.

"Oh no," she heard Alyssa mutter. "You've got to be kidding me."

"What?" Madison tried to glance behind her to see what was going on, but the bike lurched. "Are you okay? Did a bug fly in your mouth? Do you need to stop?"

"No. I was just thinking … maybe we shouldn't go to Shop & Save."

"Why not?"

"There seems to be a crowd over there, and the lineups are going to be terrible. Is there somewhere else we can go to pick up that cheese and the butter your dad needs?"

Madison looked down the street. Sure enough, a huge mob of people was milling around behind a roadblock, and big trucks lined the curb with weird apparatus being unloaded from them. "Oh my god," she breathed, coasting to a stop and looking back at Alyssa. "The TV show. Oh my god. Oh my god!"

"Stop saying that," Alyssa said and scowled. "You sound like a scratched CD."

"No, you don't understand, Lyssa," Madison

said, waving her arms around excitedly. "This is super cool! The TV people are in town. They're shooting, right here! I'm sure it's them. What else could it be?" She straightened the bike and tried to push off, but the bike didn't budge. "Wha ..." She looked down. Alyssa's feet were still firmly planted on the ground. "Lyssa," she said with a laugh. "You have to lift your feet or the bike won't go. Ready, on the count of three. One ... two ... three!" The bike wobbled again, but Madison had a good grip on the handles and was able to keep it upright.

Madison pedalled toward the store, her heart racing, tingly chills dancing up and down her spine. The TV people were here. Unbelievable! Maybe they'd even get to watch them shoot, or get an autograph. She pulled her bike to a stop at the fringe of the crowd and the girls dismounted.

Joey Rodriguez ran by, his arms outstretched, swooping his cell phone through the air like a plane. "Whoohoo! I got my picture taken with Jessica Ashton herself. She put her arm around me and everything!"

"Did you hear that?" Madison clutched Alyssa's arm. "Jessica Ashton is *here!*"

"Whatever," Alyssa said.

"You must not have seen her in anything.

Otherwise you'd be pooping yourself," Madison exclaimed, wheeling her bike to a lamppost and winding her lock around it. "I wish my mom wasn't so old-fashioned." She snapped the lock shut. "I'm sure cell phones don't cause cancer. Everyone has one but me. And now here we are, a TV star on our doorstep, and we can't get a picture. Wait! Do you have your cell phone?"

"Not with me."

"Phooey." Madison sighed. "Oh well, we'll just have to take a picture with our minds then. Come on." She grabbed Alyssa's hand. "Let's try to get closer so we can see the action." She started weaving her way through the throng. Alyssa seemed to be hanging back a bit. "It's okay," Madison said over her shoulder. "Don't be shy."

"Quiet on the set, we are *roll*ing!" Madison heard a man call out. Suddenly everybody stood still and stopped talking. Madison wished they were closer to the front. All she could see were the backs of people and the big red Shop & Save sign on the top part of the brick building.

"Speed," another man called out.

"*Action!*" a third voice barked.

There was silence. Then came the sound of a car pulling up to the curb, a screech of tires, a car door slamming, someone running in high heels. "Help!" a woman cried. Her voice was filled with anxiety and fear. "Please help me!" she pleaded.

"Oh my god," Madison mouthed to Alyssa, who was standing stock-still. "It's her!"

"And ... cut," a man yelled. "Reset the car. We've got to go again."

Everyone started talking and moving about. Madison grabbed Alyssa's hand again and resumed manoeuvring toward the front. "That was her! I swear it. I'd know that voice anywhere. That was Jessica Ashton. You think I'm fooling? Wait till we get to the front. You'll see." She squeezed in next to Old Man Parker and his daughter, Daisy, who'd set him up comfy in a folding chair. He was decked out in his Sunday best, his sparse hair plastered down. Mr. Parker was a hundred and two, the oldest living resident of Rosedale. On his hundredth birthday, his picture had been on the front page of *The Rosedale Tribune*.

"Good afternoon, Mr. Parker, Daisy," Madison said. "Pretty exciting, huh?"

"Oh yes," Mr. Parker wheezed, nodding up and down like a bobble-head doll. "See the pretty lady standing by that Mercedes coup? She's my girlfriend."

"Is not," Alyssa muttered.

"Now, Dad, don't you be telling tall tales," Daisy admonished.

"Is too." His querulous voice was getting louder. "Right after I came back from World War Two, the world was going crazy celebrating, you see, and me and that pretty filly over there took ourselves uptown to ..."

"Quiet on the set. *Rolling*."

"Speed," a man with earphones called. He was looking down rather intently at his cart of electronic equipment, sliding a knob a little to the left.

"And ... action!" a man with a scrappy beard and curly black hair yelled. He was wearing a baseball cap set low on his head and he had earphones on. Perched on a tall wood-and-canvas folding chair, the man was staring at a monitor that was like a miniature TV—except it showed the very street they were standing on, and Madison could see the car speeding toward the camera on its screen.

"That must be the director," Madison mouthed to Alyssa.

The car skidded to a stop in front of the store and Jessica Ashton got out. She was so beautiful Madison's heart got stuck in her throat. Tears were pouring down Jessica Ashton's face as she ran toward a man and his wife who were pushing a grocery cart away from the store. "Help!" she cried. "Please help me!" she wailed, clinging to the husband's arm.

"And cut!" the director shouted. Jessica Ashton and the husband and wife all relaxed. A woman darted over to Jessica and held out a Kleenex box. Jessica took a couple, wiped her face, blew her nose, and placed the used Kleenex on the clean one that the woman had covering her outstretched hand. The grocery-cart man said something under his breath and the two women laughed.

"How was it, Ted?" Jessica Ashton asked, turning to look at the director over her shoulder, her long blond hair rippling in the sun as if she were in a hair commercial.

"Fantastic, babe," the director said. "Moving on. Next shot in the park. You can go to your trailer, sweetcakes. It'll take a while to set up."

Jessica Ashton smiled and stretched, her back arching like a cat's.

"Now that's what I'm talking about," Old Man Parker said, whipping the binoculars that were hanging around his neck up to his red-rimmed, watery eyes.

"Dad ..." Daisy admonished again. But he just cackled and kept the binoculars right where they were.

"Excuse me, Jessica Ashton, over here!" a tall girl to the left of Madison called, waving her arms vigorously in the air. She looked like she was in high school or maybe even university. "Miss Ashton, please, can I have your autograph?"

Jessica Ashton started to amble over to where the barricades were set up. Madison felt a tug on her arm. "Let's go," Alyssa said.

"Are you kidding? This is our big chance to meet a real live TV star!"

"I don't want to."

"Don't be scared," Madison said, turning to look at her friend. "She's not going to bite."

"I'm not scared," Alyssa said through gritted teeth.

"Alyssa?" Madison heard a velvety rich voice behind her. She turned slowly around, her heart pounding, and sure enough, there was Jessica Ashton in the flesh, standing right in front of her, smiling.

"Oh ... my ... god!" Madison croaked, goose-bumps rising. "Miss Ashton?" If she reached out her hand right now, it would touch her! Wait ... How did this TV star know Lyssa's name? Why did she pick out the two of them especially to talk to? Madison slowly turned back and looked at Alyssa, who was staring at Miss Ashton as if she were a zombie come to life.

"Hey, sweetie," Jessica Ashton drawled in her famous honey-and-cream voice. "How'd you get here? Is this the little friend you were telling me about?"

Madison's head whipped back and forth from Miss Ashton to Alyssa. "You *know* her?" she managed to croak. But the sound of her voice seemed to release Alyssa from her stupor, and she spun around and dove into the crowd.

"Oh dear," Miss Ashton said, looking rueful. "I messed that up, didn't I?"

"Excuse me, I'm sorry but I ..." Madison stammered as she plunged into the mass of people to try and catch up with Alyssa.

12
best friends
and pinky-swear

Alyssa was pretty far down the road when Madison busted free of the crowd. There was no way she'd be able to catch up with her on foot.

It took two attempts at the combination before Madison got her bike lock opened, her fingers clumsy and her mind spinning as she replayed over and over what just happened, trying to make sense of it.

She glanced up in time to see Alyssa turn right on Fairfield, which was the wrong direction and the wrong street to get back to the house. "Oh great, she's going to get lost," Madison muttered, leaping onto her bike and beginning to pedal as fast as she could.

As Madison turned onto Fairfield, she caught a flash of Alyssa's distinctive pale purple hoodie disappearing into an alley on the left. "Lyssa!" she shouted. "Wait up!"

But Alyssa was gone.

Madison's legs and lungs were burning now, but somehow she found an extra burst of energy and kicked up the speed even more. Her bike skidded out a bit as she turned into the alley. It was another dead end, so Alyssa had to be somewhere in there. "Lyssa!" Madison called as she dismounted, her legs feeling wobbly and jelly-like from pushing them so hard. She walked her bike down the alley, her gaze scanning left and right, her heart pounding in her ears. "It's me, Madison. Are you all right?" She paused for a second and listened.

Then, from behind the rusty green Dumpster, she heard a choking kind of gasp, like someone was crying hard but trying not to let any sounds escape.

Madison propped her bike against the front of the smelly Dumpster and walked cautiously around to the side. And there was Alyssa, sitting hunched with her back jammed into the corner where the Dumpster and the brick wall met, arms wrapped tightly around her knees, chin tucked down to her chest, her long blond hair making it impossible for Madison to see her face. But there was no mistaking the fact that she was crying. She must have been crying the entire time she ran away from Miss Ashton, because the front of her hair looked stringy and wet.

"Lyssa," Madison said softly, dropping to her knees beside her friend, gingerly putting an arm around her. "What's going on?"

Alyssa didn't answer, just shook her head from side to side, her shoulders shaking from the effort of holding back all that emotion.

"Lyssa, how did Jessica Ashton know your name?" At that, the floodgates opened, and Alyssa couldn't keep the sobs contained. "What's going on?" Madison asked, holding her tight. "You can tell me. It's okay."

"No, it's not," Alyssa cried. "It will never be okay."

"What won't be okay?"

Alyssa's head reared up, suddenly ferocious. "She's my mother!" Alyssa yelled, shaking Madison's arm off her shoulder, glowering at her through her hair. "She's my stupid mother, okay?" Alyssa's face was twisted up, bitter. "There, *now* are you happy?"

Madison could only stare, speechless.

"What are you gaping at me like that for? I'm not a freak. And I'm not lying either, if that's what you think."

"No ... I ... It's just ..." Madison's mind felt

like mush. Sentences weren't coming clearly. "But …" she stammered. "Your last name is Hawkins and she——"

"Ashton's her stage name. What's the diff?" Alyssa said, cutting her off.

She's really mad at me, Madison thought, but at least she wasn't crying anymore, so that was good. "So Hawkins is your dad's last name?"

"No! Jeez, I already told you I don't *have* a dad, so why would I *have* his last name?"

"I don't know, I just——"

"——Hawkins is my mom's *real* last name, the one she was born with. When she moved to Hollywood and joined the Screen Actors Guild, another Jessica Hawkins was already registered, so my mom had to change her name."

"Oh, I see," Madison said. But she didn't.

Neither girl spoke. Madison sat beside her friend on the broken asphalt, the brick wall behind them rough and slightly warm through the fabric of her shirt. An orange-striped tomcat scrambled up onto the wood fence across the alley, walked over to the corner post, sat down, hoisted his leg and began cleaning his bottom. It was funny. Madison glanced over at Alyssa to see if she'd noticed him too, but Alyssa's gaze was firmly fixed on her thumbnail that was prying the rubber sole away from her shoe. Madison's mom would kill her if she ever saw her doing that to her shoe. But that wasn't the thing that made Madison need to speak, it was the expression on Alyssa's face: hurt, lost, pinched shut but vulnerable too.

"I understand being upset about not knowing who your father is," Madison said softly. "That's really tough and I'm sorry about that."

Alyssa glanced over.

"But what I don't understand," Madison continued, "is why you'd be upset about Jessica Ashton being your mom. I think that would be one of the coolest things in the whole world."

"It's not," Alyssa said, the words so quiet they barely fell out of her mouth.

"But why?"

"Why?" Alyssa shook her head with a sad, weary kind of laugh. "Imagine what it's like to not know if someone's your real friend or not."

"I'm your friend."

"I don't mean you. Besides, you didn't know. I'm talking about other people. Take my 'best friend' in second grade, for instance. I was so happy when she wanted to be my friend. I thought she *liked* me."

"I'm sure she did—"

"No," Alyssa said, "she didn't. Turned out

her mother was a reporter for *The Hollywood Insider*. My mom's publicist was going crazy trying to find out where the leak was coming from, who was giving them insider information, how they got photos of the inside of our house. Apparently, that leak was me. Her mom would bring her over for 'play dates,' and while we were eating our cookies or whatever, she was snooping around the house, taking pictures, going through drawers. When I'd go over to her house, her mom would sit with us, read us stories, help us play dress-up, and all the while she'd talk to me, ask me questions. I thought she was nice. What an idiot I was. I had absolutely no idea what she was up to."

"But how could you?" Madison said, wishing she could do something to erase that bitter, self-loathing look from Alyssa's face.

"I should have known better—"

"You were a little kid!" Madison hadn't meant to yell, but she had. She'd startled both of them, and the cat too, who leapt into the air and disappeared over the fence with an angry swish of his tail.

Alyssa's mouth quirked into a smile in spite of herself. "Wow," she said. "You're quite ferocious."

"Well." Madison looked down at her hands, trying to find the right words to explain. "I don't like it when people say mean things about you. It makes me mad. Even if you're the one bad-mouthing yourself." She took a deep breath and continued. "Look, I think you're really great. So what if some stupid grownup behaved badly? I don't like you putting the blame on yourself. How were you supposed to know there were such awful people in the world? You were seven years old, Alyssa. *Seven*."

The two girls looked at each other. "Yeah," Alyssa said. "I guess you're right. I never thought of it that way before." She didn't seem so mad anymore, just small. She blotted her face with the back of her sleeve.

"I'm sorry that happened," Madison said.

Alyssa shrugged, tilting her head down so her chin was resting on her knees. They both sat there, thinking. "Anyway," Alyssa said, "it is what it is."

It wasn't even six o'clock, but already it was starting to get dark. The streetlights that lined Fairfield Road flickered on.

"You okay?" Madison asked.

Alyssa nodded.

"My dad's going to be wondering where we are."

"Yeah," Alyssa said. "I guess we better get over to Shop & Save." The shape of her mouth made a smile, but her eyes were still sort of cautious and sad.

"How about," Madison began, as she got to her feet, dusted off her butt, and held out her hand, "we swing by the corner grocery store on Windsor instead. We can get the cheese and butter for Dad, and I was thinking that if we have enough change left over, maybe we could pick up some chocolate chips and make chocolate-chip cookies for dessert."

"Okay," Alyssa said, taking Madison's hand, a real smile lighting her face. Chocolate-chip cookies were her absolute favourite. "That sounds good."

"All right then." Madison hoisted her friend to her feet. "We've got a plan." They approached her bike. "I don't have a headlight, so we're going to have to hoof it."

"That's fine, I like walking." They exited the alley and turned right. "Maddie . . ." Alyssa's voice was tentative. "I know you're sort of friends with Olivia and Isabelle, but I was wondering if you could not tell them about my mom? Keep it a secret?"

Madison glanced at Alyssa's downcast face. The shadows made it hard to see her expression clearly, but Madison could tell by the feeling radiating from her that this was important. "Of course," she said. "I think you're right not to tell them. Olivia is so star-struck and determined to break into show business. It might make things a little … um … awkward if they knew."

"Ha!" Alyssa kicked a pebble up the road. "That's an understatement." When they reached the pebble, she kicked it again, but this time it rolled off the asphalt. "Actually," Alyssa said, watching the pebble disappear into a bush, "if you could not tell anyone, I'd really appreciate it."

"Sure," Madison said, nodding her head. "No problem."

They walked a bit farther. Some of the houses were lit up inside and some were dark. A little fluffball of a white dog was standing on the top of a sofa barking at them through a front window. "Yikes, scary," Alyssa said. It continued barking until the girls turned the corner.

"It must suck," Madison said, "having to keep your mom a secret. No wonder it took you so long to invite me over."

The corner store was up ahead on the right, cool fluorescent light spilling out of the little windows under the eaves and the glass pane in the door.

"Well," Madison continued as they approached the store, "my lips are sealed. Pinky-swear. But sooner or later, Lyssa, someone is going to figure it out."

"Not if we're careful," Alyssa said with a relieved grin. She held out her crooked pinky. "Best friends?" she asked as the two girls locked little fingers.

"Best friends," Madison replied, a happy excitement thrumming through her. Mysterious secrets, pinky-swears, and now best friends: what could be better?

13
disappointing dad

The girls dumped the bike in the garage, headed up the back porch and into the kitchen, the cool early evening air clinging to their skin. No one was there, but Madison could hear the sound of the TV blaring in the living room. "We're back," she called, plopping the bag of groceries on the kitchen counter.

The television switched off and Madison's dad ambled in.

"Do you need these for tonight?" she asked, pulling out the butter and cheddar cheese. "Or should I pop them in the fridge?"

"Might as well leave them out," he said, tying on his apron. "I've got kielbasa and baked macaroni and cheese on the go. Just needed the cheddar to finish off the cheese sauce."

"Yum," Madison said, suddenly starving. "Sorry we took so long."

"Well," her dad said, his eyes twinkling, "I imagined you would." He took the lid off the large pot of boiling water on the stove, steam fogging up his glasses. "The whole town was burning up the phone wires. It was even on the local news."

Both girls froze in their tracks. "What was?" Madison asked, trying to keep her voice nonchalant. Did someone else notice that Jessica Ashton knew Alyssa's name? Did they make the connection?

"What was?" her dad chuckled. "Ever the jokester." He poured a glug of oil into the water. "Why do you think I sent you girls down to Shop & Save when I was perfectly capable of going myself?"

"I don't know." Madison was stalling for time. "Why?"

He poured some salt into his hand and threw it into the pot with a flourish. Around a third of it missed and skidded along the stovetop, but Madison's dad didn't notice. He was a messy cook. His food was tasty, but it always took longer to straighten the kitchen on the nights he made dinner.

"So you could see them shooting that TV show, why do you think?" He dumped half a box of macaroni noodles into the pot, causing droplets of water to splash out and hiss on the burner.

"Oh that," Madison said, avoiding Alyssa's gaze.

"Oh *that,* you say, like it was nothing." Madison's dad was now cutting up chunks of cheddar on the chopping block. "Girl, you've been obsessing about that show since day one." He tossed the cheddar in the sauce he had simmering on the stove. "Well, here was your golden chance! How was it? Were you able to get close? See anything?"

"Well ..." Madison suddenly felt sweaty. What was she supposed to do? Her dad had sent her to the store so she could see the TV show being shot. He'd thought it would be a happy surprise, a treat for her. And she *had* been excited. It was special until Alyssa flipped out, and now what? What was she supposed to tell her dad standing there beaming at her? If she admitted they'd been at the Shop & Save, he'd want to know what happened. And then what would she say? She'd never lied to him before, but she *had* promised Lyssa she wouldn't tell anyone. They pinky-swore. She couldn't break a pinky-swear, but if she said they weren't there, that would be lying. Not only that, but she'd talked with Daisy and Old Man Parker. They were friends with her grandparents and got together to play dominoes on Thursday nights. What if they said something?

"Uh ..." Madison said.

"Shop & Save? Darn!" Alyssa broke in. "I wish we'd known. We went to the corner store on Windsor."

"Uh ... yeah," Madison agreed. "We did." Which was true. They had. It wasn't really lying, so why did she feel so bad?

Her dad's face fell. "Why the heck did you go there?" he growled, turning back to the stove, adjusting the heat on the boiling macaroni. "I told you to go to Shop & Save. The Windsor store jacks up their prices so high, I'm surprised they haven't been arrested for highway robbery."

"Sorry," Madison said, looking down at her hands.

"Next time maybe you'll listen to me. Not only did you waste money, but you missed out on a great opportunity as well."

"I'm really sorry, Dad."

"Forget about it." He sighed, running an affectionate hand over her head. "Live and learn, chipmunk. Don't look so sad."

"Why is Maddie sad?" Gina asked, padding into the kitchen.

"I'm not sad," Madison snapped. Sometimes little sisters were such a pain.

"Then why did Daddy say you were?"

"Why were you eavesdropping? Don't you know that's rude?"

"I wasn't eve-dropping!" Gina said indignantly. "I just heard is all." She turned her back on Madison. "Hi, Lyssa. When did you get here?"

Alyssa laughed. "I came home with Maddie after school. We went to the store and now we're back again."

"I didn't see you."

"You were in your room."

"Oh." Gina thought about that for a while. "Are you sleeping over?"

"Yup," Alyssa replied.

"Where are you going to sleep? In my room?"

"*Our* room," Madison interjected.

"On my side?" Gina asked, her head tipping at an angle like a little bird.

"Of course not. She's going to sleep on my side. She's *my* friend. Why would she want to sleep on your side?"

"Because she's my friend, too!" Gina was starting to get shrill.

"How was kindergarten?" Alyssa asked, her voice calm and soothing. She should be a babysitter, Madison thought grudgingly. She was very good.

Gina's eyes opened wide. "Oh ... oh!" she

said, her feet dancing as if she had to go to the potty. "Guess what? Guess what?"

"Step back everyone," Madison's dad said. "Boiling water coming through." He dumped the contents of the pot into the colander in the sink, a huge cloud of steam whooshing up.

"I don't know, what?" Alyssa asked.

"I got ..." Gina announced, dragging the words out as if she were a game-show host about to reveal a fabulous prize. "A ..." She glanced around the kitchen to make sure she had everyone's undivided attention. "*Loose* tooth! Want to see?" She plunged her grubby hand into her mouth and started wiggling her top front tooth ferociously. "An iff going to come owt an da toof ferry iff comink and giffen me money!" she exclaimed around the fist in her mouth.

"Wow," Alyssa said, looking impressed.

"That's super cool, Gina," Madison said, feeling a little ashamed that she'd snapped at her earlier. She didn't know why she'd gotten so grouchy. Probably still feeling guilty about sort of lying to Dad. She glanced over at him. He was mixing the macaroni into the cheese sauce, and it smelled good. He dumped the whole thing in a casserole dish, sprinkled a mixture of grated cheese and bread crumbs on top, and popped it into the oven.

"You can wiggle my tooth if you like," Madison heard Gina offer. Madison spun around. Gina was jutting her face toward Alyssa, her fingers latched on her lips, pulling them back so that all her teeth were exposed.

Madison recoiled. "Eww … You're such a freak. Why would Lyssa want to put her hand in your slimy mouth?"

"I don't mind." Alyssa laughed, waving Madison off. "I'd be honoured to wiggle your tooth," she said, peering into Gina's gaping mouth. "Which one is it?"

"Dat one." Gina pointed into her mouth.

Madison could see Gina's baby tooth, half-hanging from her swollen gum. "Gross," she said, feeling squeamish.

Alyssa poked her finger and thumb into Gina's mouth, grasped the tooth, and gave it a wiggle. "Wow," she said, acting impressed. "It's *really* loose! Holy cow. This tooth could fall out at any second."

"I *know*!" Gina puffed out her chest, smiling proudly.

The front door thumped shut. There was the jingling of Madison's mom's keys as she dropped them in the ceramic bowl on the hall table. "We're in here, Kathy," Madison's dad called.

Madison's mom entered the kitchen. "Sorry I'm late." She got a glass of water from the sink and gave her husband a kiss on her way to the table. "I'll be glad when the TV people go," she said, sinking wearily into a kitchen chair and slipping off her pumps. "It was a zoo trying to get home, with roads blocked off and all that equipment."

Madison glanced over at her friend. Did it hurt her feelings when she heard things like that? Did it make her feel unwelcome, thinking people wanted her and her mom gone? "I like that they're here," Madison said. "It livens up the town, and I'm sure if we were lucky enough to get to know any of them, we'd like them a lot." She smiled at Alyssa and Alyssa smiled back. *Best friends*, Madison thought, and suddenly she didn't feel so bad about not telling her dad the whole story.

"Perhaps," her mom said, crossing her ankle over her knee so she could rub her foot. Her mom's feet were always sore when she came home from the bank: too many hours encased in her dress shoes. "Do I have time for a shower?"

"Sure," Madison's dad replied. "But don't be long, dinner's almost ready. Girls, if you could set the table?"

Madison did the silverware, one knife and

one fork each. She contemplated doubling up on the cutlery so that it would look fancier, but her family would think she'd gone bonkers. Alyssa put out the water glasses. Gina managed to open the drawer and get the paper napkins with one hand while the other continued to wiggle her tooth.

By the time Madison's mom returned, wearing her worn terry-cloth robe, her wet hair wrapped in a towel, Madison's stomach was singing hosannas. Her dad slid the bubbling baked macaroni and cheese and the kielbasa out of the oven. They got their plates served up, mouths watering. All that biking had made Madison super hungry. For the next ten minutes there wasn't much conversation, just the sound of forks and knives scraping on plates, tasty food being lifted to mouths, people chewing. Every once in a while someone would say "Umm ..." or "Delicious ..." or "You did it again ..."

Madison and Alyssa were at the counter getting seconds when Gina let out an ear-piercing shriek, rocketing to her feet. "What the heck?" Madison exclaimed, so startled that the spatula dropped out of her hand, splattering the floor with a gooey cheesy mess.

"My tooth!" Gina cried.

"What about it? Sheesh, so you've got a loose

tooth. It's going to hurt a bit when you chew."
But Gina didn't answer. She just stood in shock,
her finger pointing into her mouth. It was then
that Madison noticed the gaping hole. "You lost
it!" Madison gasped.

"Holy cow!" Alyssa crowed. "That's so cool,
Gina."

Both girls rushed over to Gina, crowding
around. Madison's dad reached over and took
her mom's hand. "Our little girl is growing up,"
he said.

"Spit it out, Gina." Madison held her hand in
front of her little sister's face. "You don't want to
swallow it by accident."

"Why?" Gina asked, her eyes wide.

"Well, I don't know. It's sharp and might
cut your intestines or something. Don't look so
worried, I'll give it right back to you."

"Cu ... cut my in ... test ... tons?" Gina
stammered, and then she burst into tears.

"No, it wouldn't," their dad said. "It would go
through your system like anything else you put
in your mouth and come out in your poop."

"Why are you trying to frighten your sister?"
Her mom looked at Madison reproachfully.

"I'm not!" Madison exclaimed. She was just
trying to help and now she was getting blamed.
"Stop crying, you might swallow it. Spit it out."

She wanted to grab her wailing sister by the shoulders and give her a shake.

"But … I can't …" Gina sobbed. "It's not there!" Her finger frantically fished around the inside of her mouth. "I must have swallowed it with a hunk of kielbasa."

"Are you sure?" their mom asked, getting out of her chair and kneeling in front of Gina. "Open your mouth, poppet, and let me take a look."

Gina opened her mouth wide as their mom ran her finger along Gina's gums, under her tongue, and behind her back teeth. Then she sighed and got to her feet. "I'm afraid Gina's right. That tooth is well and truly gone."

14
tooth drama

"We have to be really quiet," Madison cautioned, standing in the darkened hallway with her hand on her bedroom doorknob, "so Gina won't wake up." Her sister was a pretty deep sleeper, but Madison wasn't going to take any chances. It was Alyssa's first time sleeping over and she didn't want Gina messing it up.

She turned the knob slowly until she heard the soft *snick* of the latch, then she slid the door open and entered on quiet cat feet. There was a slant of light coming out from under the adjoining bathroom door. Gina must have forgotten to turn it off. What else was new? "We'll brush our teeth and wash our faces and then you can change into your pyjamas," Madison mouthed, her voice a barely-there whisper.

"Okay," Alyssa whispered back. "This is so

fun. I feel like a super sleuth." She extended her leg, pointed her toe, and started walking with giant sneaky stealth steps.

An unladylike snort escaped from Madison's nose. "You look," she said, trying to suppress a fit of giggles, "like a cartoon character when you walk like that." Which didn't help matters, because Lyssa revved up the walk to ridiculous proportions until Madison had to lunge for the bathroom to get inside before she exploded with laughter.

"*Hey!*" Gina bellowed. "I *need* privacy."

"What the *heck?*" Madison couldn't believe her eyes. There was Gina squatting on the toilet seat in a weird sort of contorted position, her naked bottom out for the world to see. One hand was hanging on to the front of the toilet seat to maintain her precarious balance. The other arm was twisted around to the back, holding something tan with dark stitching underneath her bottom. *Was that . . . ?* Madison squinted, her eyes still adjusting to the light. *No! It couldn't possibly be?! Even Gina wouldn't be that . . . OH MY GOD!*

"Gina," Madison said through gritted teeth. "You better tell me *that* is not what I *think* that is."

"Get out. Get out!" Gina squawked. "I'm doing business here!"

"If that's my baseball mitt, *you* are *dead!*"

There was a brief second where their eyes locked, Madison's narrowing into tiny slits and Gina's getting larger and larger.

"MOMMY!" Gina hollered at the top of her lungs. "HELP!" She leapt off the toilet, the baseball mitt held in front of her like a platter of meat. "HELP ME!" she bleated as she darted past a lunging Madison.

"Catch her!" Madison yelled, but when Gina sprinted past, Alyssa was no help at all. "Alyssa!"

"I'm sorry … I'm sorry," she gasped, sliding down the wall, clutching her stomach. "Oh my god." Alyssa was laughing so hard tears were streaming down her face. "She was …," Alyssa choked out, "… carrying a little brown turd in your mitt."

"MOM!" Madison bellowed. "MOM!"

"I'm right here," Madison's mother said, appearing at the girls' bedroom door. Gina darted behind her and hung on to her legs.

"She," Madison said, thrusting her finger at her little sister, "*pooped* in my catcher's mitt."

"Gina?" Their mother looked down at her younger daughter. "Is this true?" She was using her deep calm parental voice, but Madison could see that the corners of her mouth were twitching.

"It's not funny, Mom! I use that mitt all the time. What kind of wackadoodle poops in her sister's baseball glove, for crying out loud?"

Madison's father's head appeared over her mother's shoulder. "What's all the ruckus?" he asked.

"She *pooped*, in my——" Madison started to explain, but in the middle of her sentence, she was interrupted by a loud snort of laughter that erupted from her mom's nose. Her mom was laughing? "This is *not* funny!"

"I'm sorry, honey," her mother said, trying to look remorseful, but her puny effort was totally spoiled because she *was* laughing. Laughing so hard she was hanging on to the door frame for support.

Madison's dad looked from Madison to Alyssa, who was howling with laughter on the bathroom floor, then to his wife, and finally to a puzzled Gina and the object she held in the mitt. "Hmm," he said, giving her an affectionate pat on the shoulder. "It looks like we have a budding scientist on our hands."

"Dad," Madison said, "the little twerp didn't even ask."

"She didn't *ask*!" Alyssa shrieked. Both Alyssa and Madison's mother dissolved in a renewed bout of guffaws.

"It's a *catcher's* mitt," Gina explained. "I needed something good for catching."

"You had no right!" Madison shouted.

"And what were your plans for that?" their dad asked, pointing at the smelly brown object nestled in the centre of Madison's mitt.

"Sort through it and find my tooth. I was lying in bed and I couldn't sleep. I was worried that maybe the tooth fairy didn't know how to read and she would see that note Mommy wrote and wouldn't know what it said and then no tooth fairy money for me. And maybe it would be like the Boy Who Cried Wolf, and the next time I lost a tooth, she'd think, *so what*, that it was another false alarm. All my friends at school would be getting money for all their teeth and I'd have nothing. So, you see, Dad, I really need to find that tooth."

Madison's dad's gaze travelled from Gina's face to the glove and grimaced. "Now, you know, Gina, that in all likelihood, your tooth hasn't worked its way through your digestive system yet."

"But what if it has?"

"Hmm …" Their dad stroked his chin in a thoughtful sort of manner. "You've got a point there." He contemplated the situation a bit more. "Perhaps we should—"

"Eww ..." Madison knew what that expression on her dad's face meant. "Mom, please, you've got to stop them," she said, suddenly panicked. Alyssa was never going to want to come over again. She was used to TV stars and swimming pools and chauffeurs and foreign languages. It was bad enough that her stupid kid sister wanted to sort through her poop, but her father? He was a grownup! "Please, Dad," she begged. "Don't!"

"I don't see what the problem is, Madison," her father replied. "Yes, Gina shouldn't have used your mitt without permission, but the damage is done. And who knows, maybe Gina has the makings to be a scientist or a ... proctologist. I'm not going to nip these very promising signs of a scholarly mind in the bud just because of a little squeamishness." He turned back and beamed at Gina as if she'd done something clever. "How about you and I get some latex gloves from the first-aid drawer and deal with that puppy."

"Robert." Madison's mother sighed. She wasn't laughing anymore. "Really, you shouldn't encourage her."

"Nonsense, Kathy," he replied. "An inquiring mind should always be encouraged."

"I don't want that traipsing into my clean kitchen. Take her out back and I'll get the gloves."

"Thank you, my dear," he said. He put his arm around Gina's shoulder and ushered her from the room, Madison's mom following in his wake.

"Spoiled brat," Madison muttered, stalking over to the door and slamming it hard behind them. "I can't believe she didn't even get in trouble! It's not fair. She ruins my mitt and I get bawled out and *she*'s treated like she's some kind of budding scientific genius."

Madison stomped over to her bed and sat down on it, shoulders hunched, eyes squeezed shut. Her face felt like it was on fire. Why did she have such a weird, freaky family? She could hear the faint sounds of Gina's excited, high-pitched voice and her dad's low rumbling one out in the backyard by the hose. What were they doing out there? Squishing through poop. What was Alyssa thinking? She probably wouldn't want to be friends anymore. Why did this totally humiliating situation have to happen when she was here? Madison heard Alyssa get up, footsteps crossing the floor. Was she going to the kitchen to call Maximilian and tell him that she wanted to be picked up?

The footsteps stopped beside her. Madison didn't dare look at her. "Are you okay?" Alyssa asked. She felt Alyssa's hand alight on her shoulder.

"I'm so embarrassed," Madison managed to choke out.

"Why?"

"My crazy family … and especially since yours is so fancy, I wanted everything to be perfect when you stayed overnight."

"Maddie …" Alyssa knelt down beside her. Madison was too ashamed to look up, too afraid of what she'd see reflected on her friend's face. But Alyssa's voice didn't seem mocking. It was sincere, serious. "I love your family. You have no idea."

Madison glanced up. Her friend didn't look repulsed at all.

"Coming here," Alyssa continued, "for me, it's like a taste of heaven."

Suddenly Madison felt a million times lighter. "Really?"

Alyssa nodded. "Besides," she began. Her mouth twitched, and then a chuckle escaped as well. "It's not like *you're* the one out there rummaging through poop."

"No," Madison replied emphatically, and suddenly the humour of the situation struck her as well. "My sister is a nut," she gasped through gales of laughter. "I'm going to have to sterilize that mitt."

"I think," Alyssa said, putting on a posh English

accent and arching an eyebrow, "that perhaps you'll want to splurge on a new one."

"Yeah," Madison said, even though she didn't know where she'd get the money. Good baseball mitts weren't cheap.

social studies

Madison squirmed uncomfortably at her desk, twirling a piece of her almost-grown-out bangs on her finger. All around her she could hear the sound of pencils scratching out answers. It was very distracting. Madison stared at the Social Studies test in front of her. The first question—*Who lived in a fertile land and developed the first civilization in the Americas?*—she'd gotten. That was easy. The Olmec. It was the next question that had her stumped. *The Olmec civilization emerged in:*

    a. 200 CE and lasted until 1300 CE
    b. 1500 and lasted until 400 BCE
    c. 600 CE and lasted until 1200 CE

She twirled her hair a little faster. What was it? Her mind was drawing a blank. This was horrible. She was going to get an F for sure. She should have asked her dad for help. He was always great at finding ways to help her memorize things, making up funny poems or stories to tie things together.

She'd wanted to go to her dad, but ever since Alyssa slept over and they'd fudged the truth about going to Shop & Save, Madison had felt guilty around him. Like she was untrustworthy, like she had the word *Liar* tattooed across her forehead.

How long had she been sitting there, stuck? Madison glanced up at the clock. Only eight more minutes until lunch? No way was she going to finish the test in time. Her stomach growled, but luckily nobody looked up. It must not have been as loud as it seemed. "Focus, Madison," she whispered to herself, rubbing her forehead, hoping that would help stimulate her brain. *"Focus."* She stared hard at the test, squinting her eyes closer and closer until she was looking at the question through her eyelashes.

a. 200 CE and lasted until 1300 CE
b. 1500 and lasted until 400 BCE
c. 600 CE and lasted until 1200 CE

Which one? Which one? And what did CE and

BCE stand for anyway? And why didn't 1500 have either a CE or a BCE? "Oh forget it," Madison muttered, "I don't know." She let out the breath she'd been holding and circled *b.* That was a trick she'd learned from her dad. "If you don't know the answer," he'd say, "circle something anyway. A one in three chance is better odds than no chance at all, and who knows, you might get it right."

Two questions down, eight more to go. Pathetic.

Next question. *What helped the Olmec develop the first civilization in the Americas?* Well, as her grandpa would say, hell's bells. The answer to the first question was right there in the third question. *What helped the Ol ...* In a flash it came to her. Madison quickly scribbled down *trade.* She could have elaborated, but there wasn't time.

Joey Rodriguez slapped his pencil down, his hand shooting up into the air.

"Yes, Joey?" Ms. Elliot said.

"I'm finished," he announced, way louder than he needed to. "That was a cinch. Can I be dismissed for lunch?"

Sheesh. What a show-off. Madison fumed. She was just getting on a roll and bigmouth Joey had broken her concentration.

"No," Ms. Elliot answered. "The bell doesn't go for two more minutes. You can check over your work. Or sit quietly and read."

Two more minutes! No way. Next question. *What crops did the Olmec grow along the fertile land next to the rivers? Think ... think ... think! Corn ... beans ... squash ...* Madison nibbled on her pencil. *You know this: four, there were four. Corn, beans, squash, and ... what?*

"I can't read anything in two minutes," Joey complained, tipping back in his seat with his hands locked behind his head and a big grin on his face.

"Joseph Rodriguez." Ms. Elliot tapped her ruler sharply on the desk. "You are interrupting the class. Please be quiet."

Corn ... beans ... squash ...

"Oh boy," Joey chortled softly, leaning way out of his seat so that his nose was practically on Madison's shoulder. "You are in trou*ble*."

Isabelle craned her neck, trying to get a look.

"Shut up, Joey," Madison said, her teeth clenched, covering her test with her arm.

"You are *never* going to get done."

"Shut up!"

"Ms. Elliot," Alyssa called, raising her hand. "Joey is bothering us." But by the time Ms. Elliot glanced up from the papers she was correcting,

Joey was sitting upright in his desk with his hands folded in front of him and an angelic expression on his face. Isabelle giggled.

"Joseph," Ms. Elliot said and sighed. "I don't want to have to speak with you again."

The lunch bell sounded. "Please leave your tests on my desk on your way out," Ms. Elliot said to the class. "Don't forget to write your name in the top right-hand corner. Have a good lunch." Everyone surged toward the teacher's desk, laughing and chatting.

"Did you forget to study?" Olivia asked, pausing at Madison's desk, her face oddly sympathetic.

"No." Madison shook her head. "I studied."

"Come on, Olivia," Isabelle said, tugging her arm. "Let's go." The girls joined the rush of students tumbling out of the room.

Madison slowly wrote her name on her paper. She felt sick. This was the worst she'd ever done on a test. Reluctantly, she brought her paper to the front. "I'm sorry," she said as she slipped it into the middle of the pile. "I didn't do very well."

"Not to worry," Ms. Elliot replied. "That was a practice test. You'll get another chance on Monday."

"We will?" Madison asked. "Honest?"

Ms. Elliot smiled. "Certainly. It's a lot to remember. Generally it takes a little time to get it all straight, unless, of course, you're a history buff like Joey."

Alyssa was waiting for Madison by her cubby. "How did you do?" she asked.

"Terrible." Madison grimaced, grabbing her lunch bag and heading out into the hall. "We get another shot at it next Monday, but I don't know. I studied really hard for this test and still I did lousy. It's like all the information got jumbled up in my head and became a big gooey mush pile."

"Speaking of a big gooey mush pile," Alyssa said with a grin, "did your little sister ever ... ahem ... find her tooth?"

"Don't remind me," Madison groaned, rolling her eyes. "Yes, she did."

"And the tooth fairy, did she ...?" Alyssa raised an eyebrow.

"Uh ... huh." Madison nodded. "Oh yeah, apparently the tooth fairy isn't picky." Both girls laughed, pushed the bar on the door, and stepped outside.

It had rained that morning, but the fast-moving wind had separated the clouds to allow shafts of sunlight to stream through. "Ah ... How beautiful." The girls shut their eyes and breathed in deep.

"I can smell ..." Madison said, searching with her senses, "... fresh wet pine needles."

They took another long breath, their eyes still shut.

"I can smell," Alyssa said, in a romantic dreamy voice, "the stench from the garbage can on our left. Rotting apple cores, moulding sandwiches—"

"Alyssa," Madison laughed, opening her eyes and giving her friend a gentle whack on the arm. "That's not what you're supposed to notice."

"Why not?" Alyssa grinned back at her. "It's what I smelled."

"You know what I mean."

"Madison," Alyssa said, putting on a solemn, enlightened voice. "As my mother always says, there is light and there is shadow. One cannot exist without the other. To deny one causes imbalance in the universe—"

"Wowee, Mad-one. You did terrible in there," Joey said, dribbling a basketball past them, dodging this way and that as if a slew of six-foot-six basketball players were in pursuit. He spun on his heel, arched in the air, and flipped the basketball over his shoulder to his friend Dylan. It was a glorious move that reminded Madison of fly-fishing with her dad, and how when the fish were feeding, they'd propel their entire bodies out of the water, glinting in the soft first rays of the early morning sun.

Joey's move took Dylan by surprise, however, and Dylan wasn't able to get his hands up before the ball went whizzing by him.

"Nice move, Showy Joey," Alyssa replied, tipping her nose in the air and tossing her long blond hair over her shoulder.

"Yeah," Madison said. "Real smooth."

"Mad-one had zippo done on her test. Fail city for sure."

"I had some done," Madison protested.

"Oh sure," Joey cackled. "Like three out of ten. Hoowee, are you dumb."

"She is not, Joey Rodriguez," Alyssa said, poking him in the chest with her forefinger. "She is super smart." Alyssa sure was getting feisty on her behalf. Madison felt lucky to have such a good best friend.

"Oh yeah?" Joey drawled.

"Oh yeah. How do you make chocolate-chip cookies?"

"Say what?" Joey looked confused.

"You don't know how? Well, Madison does. She can make cookies that blow your socks off. How do you spell *invigorate?*"

"Huh?" The conversation was obviously not going the way Joey had anticipated.

"Madison?" Alyssa said, gesturing magnanimously toward her as if she were the long-legged beauty on a game show revealing what was behind curtain number one.

"I-N-V-I-G-O-R-A-T-E. Invigorate," Madison said with a grin.

"I rest my case," Alyssa said, taking Madison's arm. "Shall we?"

"Certainly," Madison said, and the two of them strolled away, leaving Joey standing there stunned, arms dangling at his sides, his mouth gaping open.

16
scrabble

Madison leaned forward on her cushion and scooped another handful of roasted cashews from the dainty china bowl painted with pink flowers and a thin ribbon of gold around the fluted top. Cashews were her favourite nut, but she always made sure to take only a few at a time. She didn't want to seem greedy. Cashews were delicious, but they were also super expensive and her grandparents were not exactly rolling in dough.

"Hmm ..." her grandpa said, scowling at the little wooden letters propped up in front of him, his bushy eyebrows looming over the thick lenses of his bifocals.

Madison took a nibble of another cashew, shutting her eyes to savour it. Yum. It tasted so good. With her eyes still shut, she put the rest of the cashew in her mouth and crunched it slowly. She could hear the *click ... click ... click ...* as her grandpa moved his Scrabble letters around on his rack. Their cat, Sadie, indulged in a final chorus of chest-rumbling purrs that slowly wound down to silence as she drifted off into a contented sleep. Madison's fingers played through the cat's fur; she enjoyed the feeling of Sadie's fat warm body snuggled up next to her.

"Damn vowels," her grandpa muttered. "Nothing but vowels. Feast or famine." *Click ... click ... click.* "Well, I guess this will have to do."

Madison opened her eyes and watched as he leaned forward from the sofa and placed his tiles. H-U-I-P-I-L. "Huipil," he said, cracking his knuckles, then leaning back and draping his long lanky arm along the top of the sofa.

"Huipil?" Madison squinted at him suspiciously.

"What?" he said, a little too casually. "You think maybe I made it up?" He slid a quick, sneaky glance at her.

"You've been known to do it." Madison tapped her tooth with her pen.

He shrugged. "Why don't you challenge me then?" he suggested in a mild-mannered tone, all innocent, but Madison caught a flash of glee in his eyes.

"Nope," she said, sliding the grey letters bag across the coffee table. "I trust you, Grandpa. Choose your letters." In Scrabble it was important to be able to read one's opponent. *Huipil* was a word all right. Madison had never heard of it, but she could tell that her grandpa was trying to sucker her into thinking it wasn't, so he'd get an extra turn. He was a ruthless Scrabble player. "How many points is that?"

He sighed heavily. "You're a hard woman to beat, Madison my dear." His long knobby forefinger tapped the tiles he'd laid down on the board. "Four ... one ... The *I* is on the triple letter score, so that's three more, plus three for the *P*, and then one and one." He sighed again. "It's a measly thirteen points. Are you sure you don't want to challenge me?"

"Positive," Madison replied, adding thirteen points to his score. "I don't know what you're complaining about. You already have two hundred and forty-six points. What does *huipil* mean?"

"It's an embroidered Mexican dress or blouse. Quite pretty things," he said, reaching over and snagging one of the store-bought chocolate-coated peppermint cookies off the plate that Grandma had set on the coffee table. "Why, if I had a million dollars, I'd fly down to Mexico myself to buy you and your sister one. Speaking of daydreams, Davy Parker said he saw you down at Shop & Save chatting with a TV star."

"What?" Madison said, her mouth suddenly dry. She ducked her head down, pretended to study the Scrabble board.

"I didn't know whether to believe him or not. Davy's mind isn't all that it used to be. Still a damn fine domino player, though." Her grandpa scooped up a handful of cashews, rattled them around in his hand like dice, and then threw a few into his mouth. "But then his daughter, Daisy, concurred, and there's certainly nothing wrong with *her* brain."

Madison shifted her tiles around uneasily. She could hear the low murmur of her dad and grandma in the kitchen. He was setting up a computer to help his parents "step into the twenty-first century" and get online.

"Anyway," her grandpa continued. Madison wished he'd keep his voice down. What if her dad heard him? "They claim that this Jessica Appleton—"

"Ashton," Madison heard herself say. *Oh no!* Why did she say that? Now he'd know that she knew what he was talking about. Her cheeks felt like they were burning up. It was bad enough that she'd misled her dad about not seeing the

TV show being filmed, but now what? Was she supposed to lie to her grandpa, too? Why did she promise Alyssa that she wouldn't tell anyone?

"Eh?" her grandpa cupped a liver-spotted hand around his leathery ear. "What was that?"

"Ashton," she repeated, only upping the volume of her voice a tiny bit. "Her name is Jessica Ashton," she said, darting a quick glance at the white swinging door that led to the kitchen.

"Speak up," her grandpa said, starting to get grumpy. "Why are you whispering, girl?"

What should she do? Her hands felt clammy, her underarms moist. Madison decided to try to brazen it out. She plastered a big smile on her face. "Why you sly old fox!" Madison wagged a finger at him. "You have no shame, trying to distract me from winning the game with famous TV star talk."

"They said she walked right over and spoke directly to you."

"Shush now," Madison said, giving him a mock stern look. "I'm trying to come up with a word."

"Daisy said that the TV star seemed to know the girl you were with."

Changing the subject didn't seem to be working. Now what? Madison took a deep breath. "They must have gotten me mixed up with somebody else, because really, Grandpa, do

you suppose I'd be spending my Sunday afternoon sitting here playing Scrabble with you if I
had fancy TV star friends to hang out with?" She
had crossed that invisible line. It was no longer
a case of leaving something unsaid. She had just
lied to her grandpa, plain and simple. Her throat
felt tight, her eyes hot and blurry. She swiped at
them with the back of her arm, then switched
her *R* tile and her *D* one. What kind of person
was she turning into? Even with her head tipped
down, she could feel her grandpa's beady eyes
taking in everything.

"Oh," she exclaimed, pretending surprise,
even though she'd already figured out her
word during her grandpa's turn. "Here's a
good one." The *W* was still wide open. "*Re …
wind …*" She slowly laid her tiles down. "And
the *D* lands on the pink double-word square so
I get to double it up, and that makes twenty!"
Her voice sounded so forced, high and tinny.
She didn't dare raise her gaze to her grandpa's
face. "Yay," she said.

The living room was quiet. She could feel
him looking at her. She didn't move, just sat
staring at her upturned palms in her lap.

He cleared his throat. "Madison," he said.
"What's going on?"

She felt like she was going to cry. "I'm sorry,

Grandpa," she said in a small voice. "I can't tell. It's a secret. I promised."

"Hmm ..." he said.

The kitchen door swung open and her dad and grandma entered the living room.

"Well, your father has my computer all set up," her grandma said, wiping her hands on her flowered apron. "How's the game going?"

Madison felt slightly dizzy-headed. Was her grandpa going to say something? Was Alyssa's secret going to be safe? She glanced at him through her overgrown bangs that had fallen forward. His face looked serious, deep in thought. "The game's going fine," Madison said, her voice coming out a little squeaky.

Her dad grabbed a cookie, flopped on the sofa, and flung his arm around Grandpa's shoulder. "What's the long face for, Pop?" he asked.

Madison's grandpa looked at her long and hard. "Oh, nothing," he finally said, shaking his head. "Nothing at all."

17
father worries

The knot in Madison's stomach hadn't abated. She glanced over at her dad. They were walking home from Grandma and Grandpa's house, and so far he hadn't said a word. For some dads this would be usual. Olivia's dad didn't talk much, at least not whenever Madison and Isabelle had slept over. But Madison's dad wasn't like that, and they'd always chat when returning from his parents' house. But today his brow was furrowed as though he was deep in thought. Did he overhear her conversation with Grandpa? Was she in trouble? The silence was getting to her.

"Is everything okay?" Madison asked.

Her dad glanced over and then stopped in the middle of the sidewalk. "Did you notice anything different when you were playing Scrabble with Grandpa?"

"Different like what?"

"I don't know," her dad said, shaking his head, taking off his glasses and trying to rub out the smears with the bottom of his T-shirt. "There's something wrong. I could feel it the minute I stepped into the living room. Like he's worried and is hiding something."

"Oh," Madison said, a wave of guilt flooding over her.

"Maybe he's sick. He went to the doctor last week," her dad continued. "He said it was just a routine physical, but maybe it wasn't. Maybe something's wrong and he's too proud to say."

"Dad," Madison said, putting her hand on his arm. "Grandpa's fine. I'm sure he is. He kicked my butt at Scrabble. What's that you always say? Don't borrow trouble? Well, you're borrowing it. Grandpa's good, you'll see. Call and check for yourself when we get home."

Her dad blinked, nodded, and placed his spectacles back on his nose. "You're right," he said. "Of course." He cleared his throat. "I don't know why I ... uh ..." He straightened. "Well. One thing's for certain, I've got one hell of a smart daughter." He gave Madison a hug. She felt his kiss graze the top of her head. "Thanks, honey," he said. And she felt like the worst daughter in the world.

That night, as Madison lay in bed, she thought about her dad and how important he was to her and how much she loved him. She thought about her grandpa and how he'd kept her secret, and how her dad had gotten worried because he loved his dad, too. She thought of Alyssa, not knowing her dad. And if she didn't know her dad, that must mean that she didn't know her grandma and grandpa from her father's side of the family either! And suddenly Madison felt the weight of Alyssa's loss land on her, knocking her breath from her chest.

The door of her bedroom cracked open, and the fixture in the hall cast a long spear of light into the dark room. "Maddie?" her dad whispered. "Are you awake?"

"Yeah," she whispered back, hastily wiping her eyes.

He came into the room, a shadow shape until he got close and she could see his face through the darkness.

"I talked to Grandpa." His voice was low so he wouldn't wake up Gina. "You were right. He's fine. Everything's okay. Wanted to let you know," he said, kissing her forehead and tucking her in.

Madison was thankful he wasn't worried anymore. "Daddy," she said, catching his hand as he started to straighten. "If someone didn't know who their parents were, is there some way they could find out?"

"Why do you ask?" She could see the silhouette of his head tip to the side. She could feel the calluses on his hands, such a different feeling from her mom's. "Is this a project for school?"

Madison hesitated, because even though she'd only promised not to tell anyone about Alyssa's mother, Alyssa probably wouldn't want Madison to go blabbing about her father either. "Um … yeah. I'm writing a story about a boy who doesn't know who his … um … mom was. And now I'm stuck," she said, uncomfortable with how easily that lie rolled off her lips, grateful it was dark.

"Research! Ah … ha! That's very good. Details are what make the difference between average and excellent! Well, let's see … first off, your boy would need to know what city and state he was born in. Then he could write to the state's Office of Vital Records and request a birth certificate."

"What would that do?"

"Generally, both parents are named on a birth certificate. If you looked at your own birth certificate, you'd see your mother's name and my name too."

"I didn't know that," Madison said. "Thanks, Dad."

"Glad to help." It was dark, but she could tell by his voice that he was beaming at her. "I'm proud of you, honey."

Madison didn't answer. Couldn't. His misplaced pride in her was sitting like a rock in her gut.

After he left, she got out of bed, slipped her backpack off the back of the chair, and went into the bathroom. Once the door was shut, she turned on the light, got out her binder and a pen, and wrote *City, state born, office of vital records, birth certificate.* Then she put everything back in her pack, switched off the light, and once her eyes adjusted to the dark, made her way across the room and got back into bed.

She thought it would take a long time to fall asleep, her mind spinning with the events of the day. But it must not have, because the next thing she knew, her alarm clock was going off, morning light was streaming in through the window, and it was time to get up and ready for school.

18
research

Madison and Alyssa were in the library with the rest of their class. Everyone was supposed to be doing research for their science projects on Parts of a Plant. They'd chosen a computer at the very back in the corner, both their chairs crammed into the one cubicle. "Okay," Madison said. "Here it is. Got your pen and paper ready?"

"Check," Alyssa answered.

"With your request include as much as you can of the following: the full name of the person listed on the certificate, that would be you, *date of birth, place of birth, full name of father—"*

"But we don't know," Alyssa said, sounding panicky. "That's why we're doing this."

"It's okay," Madison replied. "It says *as much as you can*—there's nothing about how you have to have everything."

"But what if——"

"It's worth a try, right? This way, when you're eighty, you won't be sitting on your sofa with a bunch of regrets saying, I wish I'd written to that Office of Vital Records."

The tension seeped out of Alyssa's face. She laughed and picked up her pen, getting ready to write. "Good point. What else?"

"You need: *full maiden name of mother, your relationship to the person whose certificate you are requesting, the reason for your request, your address ...* I was thinking maybe we should use my address?"

Alyssa's eyes widened. She nodded. "Absolutely. Good call."

Madison shrugged like it was no big deal, but inside, she felt proud. She turned back to the computer. *"And signature and a fifteen-dollar money order."*

"Right. Got it," Alyssa said, writing it down.

"Do you know what a money order is?"

"No, but I'll figure it out. Is that all?"

"Yes. That's it. You write the letter and I'll copy down the mailing address for the Vital Records office."

"Okay." Alyssa scooted over to the next cubicle.

It didn't take Madison long to copy the address. She tipped back in her chair. It was a good feeling to help her friend. She glanced over at Alyssa, whose bottom lip was caught between her teeth as she typed away. Madison looked around the library. Isabelle and Olivia were doing a project together. Joey and Dylan weren't, but Dylan was in Joey's cubicle, and from the way they were cackling, Madison knew they weren't doing research.

Madison looked back at the glowing computer in front of her. She needed to get started on her science project, but she still hadn't settled on a plant. She knew she wanted to do one of the Oregon wildflowers she'd seen on the hikes she'd taken with her grandpa. He used to hike with her grandma, but Grandma's hip had been giving her trouble, so this summer Madison had stepped in as his hiking buddy. They'd pack a lunch, and Grandpa would grab the old gnarled stick he'd found in the woods a few years back. He'd stripped the bark off it and sanded and oiled it until its burnished wood gleamed. He called it a walking staff, and sometimes, when he and Madison were hiking, she would imagine he had flowing white hair and a beard and that he was a wizard and she was his apprentice. And sometimes it really did feel like that, when he would stop and point at a plant or a butterfly or a rock with his staff and tell her about it. He had a knack for knowing just where to look to find a patch of sweet wild strawberries or blackberries, warmed by the sun.

But as much as Madison enjoyed eating those berries, she'd decided to do a wildflower for her science project. She had narrowed it down to two of her favourites, Fireweed and Wild Blue Flax.

"Okay," Alyssa said, interrupting Madison's thoughts. "I've finished." There was a quiet triumph in her voice. She looked at Madison and grinned. "It seemed so daunting, but once we figured out what to do, it wasn't that hard."

"Great." Madison smiled back at her. "All that's left is to get a money order, mail it, and then wait."

There was a contented silence. Alyssa sighed. "Well, guess we better get to work on our science projects."

"Yeah."

"See ya." Alyssa disappeared behind the partition.

Madison turned back to her computer and typed *Fireweed* into the search box.

"I wonder," Alyssa said, leaning back so her head was peeking around the partition again, "if we Googled my mom, whether there'd be any information on who she was dating when she got pregnant with me."

"I don't know. It was a long time ago, but maybe," Madison said. "You're ten, right? When's your birthday?"

"Valentine's Day."

"Oh my god, that is like the most perfect birthday for you!"

Alyssa smiled, like she was sort of embarrassed, but pleased, too.

"So your mom would have gotten pregnant ... Okay, February plus three months is ... May. That would mean ..." Madison scrubbed her face. "Arrgh. This is complicated. Would that be eleven years ago then? Or ten?"

"I think it would be eleven," Alyssa said.

"Okay, let's give it a go." Madison typed in *Jessica Ashton* and the correct year, then clicked *search*.

A page filled with a younger Jessica Ashton popped up. "Whoa," Alyssa said, recoiling slightly.

"Wow." Madison shook her head. "It says there are five hundred and sixty-eight *thousand* results. They can't all be for that time, but still, it's going to take us ages to slog through them all. Well, no time like the present." Madison clicked on a site and a gorgeous picture of a young, super-glamorous Jessica Ashton filled the screen.

Alyssa scrunched down as if she suddenly

felt vulnerable and wanted to disappear. "You know," she said in a half whisper, "maybe we shouldn't—"

"Oh my gosh," a voice squealed. "Will you look at that! Where did you find that picture?" Madison didn't even have to turn around. She knew that voice.

Alyssa froze. Madison could see the colour literally drain out of her face.

"Isabelle, come look at this!" Olivia said, pushing between Alyssa and Madison. "I love her *so* much. Jessica Ashton is so, SO beautiful!"

Isabelle crowded around their computer, too. "Oh my god. Oh my god. Can you imagine how it would feel to look like that?" she said, doing an excited dance. "I've never seen this photo of her. We've got to print it off! Excuse me, please, can you move out of the way?"

Alyssa scooted back a bit, a dazed, trapped look in her eyes. "Sorry," Madison mouthed, as Isabelle hit the print button.

Olivia started scrolling down. "I wonder what other pictures they have?" she said.

"Girls?" Ms. Elliot's voice broke in. All four girls swivelled around.

Ms. Elliot was standing behind them, hands on her hips and a stern frown on her face. "Just what do you think you're doing?"

19
detention

"All right, girls," Ms. Elliot said, glancing up from the papers she was marking to the clock on the wall. "Detention's over. You can go. I hope you've learned your lesson."

"Yes, Ms. Elliot," Madison, Alyssa, Isabelle, and Olivia said in unison, eyes downcast as they gathered their lunches and shuffled out of the classroom.

The rest of the kids were already outside. The hall was deserted. There was the sound of someone stapling something in room 106, and the chatter of voices farther down the hall, from the staff room where the teachers ate their lunch. Madison had never had detention before, and she was pretty sure none of the other girls had either. It was an odd feeling.

They walked down the hall in silence, Olivia

and Isabelle a little in front. Isabelle pushed open the door, and the blast of autumn air seemed to unhinge her mouth. She turned and glared at Madison and Alyssa. "Thanks a lot," she said.

Madison stopped in her tracks, not sure if she was hearing correctly. "What?"

"Don't you play innocent! If it wasn't for you guys slacking off, looking up TV stars, none of this would have happened. Detention! If my mother finds out, she's going to kill me and it'll be your fault."

"*Our* fault?" Madison said.

"I wish you'd never moved here," Olivia said, glaring at Alyssa. "You're nothing but trouble!"

"Are you kidding me?" Madison sputtered. "You were the ones who——"

Olivia and Isabelle flounced out the door before she could finish. Madison lunged forward, ready to do battle, but Alyssa's hand arrived at the door handle first and held it shut.

"Don't," Alyssa said. "Let it go." Which was unexpected, because Alyssa was usually the one ready to dive in with a snappy comeback, a witty putdown.

Madison turned, saw her friend's face, and swallowed. "Okay," she said, letting go of the door. Neither girl spoke. They waited a few minutes before they pushed through the doors.

The bright sunlight made them squint.

"Whoo ... hoo! Watch out," Joey yelled, dodging past them. "It's the *bad* girls. Ohhh! Detention. Whatcha trying to do? Steal my title of *detention king?*"

"Yeah," Dylan said, zipping past. But Dylan didn't have Joey's dodging ability and banged Alyssa's shoulder.

Normally it was the kind of thing she'd shrug off. But today she just stood there looking hurt, as if she thought he'd done it on purpose.

"Get lost," Madison yelled, taking Alyssa's arm. "You guys are so immature!" But the boys just laughed as they disappeared around the side of the building, Madison's insult like water rolling off a duck's back.

"How was school?" Madison's mom asked as the family sat down around the dinner table.

Madison's gaze darted from her mother to her father. She swallowed hard. Did they know? Had Ms. Elliot called her parents?

"Grrrreat," Gina piped up like the tiger in the sugar cereal commercial. "I got an A+ on my spelling test. C-A-T spells *cat*, B-A-T spells *bat,* R-A-T spells *rat,* and M-A-T spells *mat!*"

"Wow," Madison said, relieved for once that Gina was such an attention hog. "That's really good, Gina! I'm impressed. Isn't that good, Mom?"

"Yes, that's great, Gina."

"Good job, kid," their dad said, ruffling Gina's hair. "Keep up the good work."

"I will," Gina said, her legs swinging, smiling proudly.

"And how about you?" their mom said, turning to Madison. "How was your day?"

"Um ..." Madison said, a sudden lump in her stomach. "Fine. You know ..." She shrugged, trying to appear nonchalant. "Okay." She shovelled up a forkful of mashed potatoes and stuck them in her mouth. She could feel her parents' eyes on her, but she just chewed like they were the best mashed potatoes she'd ever had. "Yum," she said enthusiastically, and then stuffed another forkful in her mouth.

fort building

"Were you able to get the money order?" Madison asked, shaking the blanket so that it flapped up and outward.

Alyssa tried to catch the other end, but missed. "Yeah, it was actually pretty easy. Max took me to the bank, I got the money order, then he drove me to the post office and I mailed it."

"Did you tell him what it was for?" Madison shook the blanket again.

"Oh, no," Alyssa said, lunging for the blanket and catching it this time. "Of course not. Why would I do that?"

Madison shrugged. If she asked her dad to help her get a money order, she was pretty sure she'd have to explain why.

"You know what I was thinking?" Alyssa said, stretching a portion of the blanket over the back of a chair. "We should be broken dead dolls for Halloween."

"Broken dead dolls?" Madison plucked a couple of heavy books from the shelf.

"I think it would be super cool! Sweet little dolls with a twist—you know, pasty white face makeup, with everything smeared a bit, dark shadows around the eyes."

"Oh yeah," Madison said, feeling the excitement rising in her belly. "That would be great. We could be splattered with blood and have wounds and a black eye and stuff. It would be the best! Nobody else is going to be a broken dead doll, that's for sure."

"Of course not. We are nothing if not original," Alyssa said with a grin.

Madison laughed. "Okay," she said. "It's a plan." She secured the last section of blanket onto the seat of the kitchen chair with the big Oxford dictionary and a thesaurus. "You can let go now," she told Alyssa.

The two girls stepped back and admired their handiwork. "The fort doesn't look like much," Madison said, examining the rather lumpy assemblage they had erected in the middle of Madison and Gina's bedroom. They'd used kitchen chairs to make the structure and draped sheets and blankets over them, which they'd pinned in place with stacks of heavy books. "But just wait until you get inside."

"I think it looks good," Alyssa said, her eyes sparkling.

"And now"—Madison waved her hands over the fort like a magician—"for the finishing touches." Both girls grinned. "You get some juice boxes and anything else you want from the fridge."

"And the candy we bought ..."

"Yeah, we don't want to forget that. And while you're collecting the supplies, I'll finish up the inside."

"This is *so* fun," Alyssa said on her way out of the room.

Madison's quilt was the floor of the fort and already in place. The first thing they'd done was spread it out; then they'd built the walls and roof around its perimeter.

Madison grabbed the pillows off her bed and a stack of her mom's old Archie comics from the bookshelf. Even though Archie comic books were sold at the store, she and Alyssa liked reading these old ones best.

The comics were well worn, and age had made the pages turn the colour of pale tea. It was funny to think of her mom poring over these comics when she was Madison's age. Just the thought of her mom having a crush on that goofy, red-haired, freckle-faced Archie made Madison smile.

On the heels of that thought came an image of Joey. Not that Madison had a crush on him. He was cute and all, but no, she didn't have a crush on him.

Get to work, she told herself. She lifted the flap of blanket, shoved the pillows and comics in as far as her arms would reach, and then crawled inside, careful not to knock the roof or the sides of the fort. She set up the comics under the legs of a chair, which made a cute cupboard. She fluffed the pillows in a comforting heap in the corner and crawled back out. Then she got the emergency flashlight from her bedside table and borrowed Gina's flashlight as well.

It wasn't an emergency, but what was a fort without flashlights? Flashlights made everything so much more fun. She was placing them in another chair cupboard when she heard the thump of feet running down the hall and then the door bump open. She hoped it was Alyssa and not pesky Gina wanting to barge in on the fun. Mom had promised to keep her occupied, but with Gina, even the best plans could get messed up.

"I've got the stuff," she heard Alyssa say, and Madison let out the breath she didn't know she was holding.

"Great, come on in."

Madison heard her walk to the entryway. The flap lifted, flooding the inside of the fort with light. Alyssa crawled in, and the flap fell back into place behind her.

When Madison's eyes adjusted to the shift in light, she could see Alyssa coming toward her. She had a juice box held upward in each palm and the sack of candy swinging gently from her gripped teeth.

"Not bad, huh?" Madison said.

"Not bad?" Alyssa said, letting the candy bag drop from her teeth. "Are you kidding me? This is totally the coolest thing I have ever done in my entire life!"

A rush of warm pleasure washed over Madison. "You're the best friend I ever had," she heard herself say, and suddenly she felt embarrassed. Maybe she shouldn't have blurted that out. She was glad it was dark.

"Me too," she heard Alyssa say. Her voice sounded like she meant it, and Madison didn't feel uncomfortable anymore.

"Candy," she bellowed, and Alyssa picked up the call.

"Candy! Candy!" they both roared as if their souls had been hijacked by a candy monster. They pounced on the bag and emptied it. Madison got out the flashlights so they could see what they were unwrapping, and then they settled down to gorge on a feast of comics and candy.

"I wonder …" Alyssa said awhile later, after they'd read a few comics and their mouths were jangly from too many sweets. "Do you think your mom would let us eat dinner in here?"

"I don't know. Maybe. I can ask." But Madison already knew what the answer would be. Her mom had a policy that the whole family had to sit down for dinner together. It was tradition.

"We should sleep here too. Do you think we'd be—"

Brrring …

"Oh, dang. My phone." Alyssa scrambled out of the fort. *Brrring …* "I'm coming, I'm coming," Madison heard her mutter. She could hear Alyssa unzip her backpack and rummage around in it.

Brrring …

"Hello?" There was a pause, then, "Do I have to?" Another pause. "Mom, I *know* you were away on location for four days. I was in that big empty house missing you. But I'm over at Madison's now and we just built this really cool fort and we were going to eat dinner in it and sleep in it and everything ..." Another pause, followed by a large sigh. "I doubt she'll want to. Okay, okay, I'll ask. What time is Max coming? *Half* an *hour*?! Mom ..." There was another pause. "Okay. Fine. Bye."

Silence.

"Lyssa?" Madison crawled out of the fort. Her friend was sitting dejectedly by her open backpack, her cell phone still in her hand. "Are you okay?"

"Yeah. I've got to go to dinner with my mom and her stupid director." Alyssa flopped to her side, her head on her backpack like a pillow. "By the way," she added, her voice gloomy, "I like where you hung my painting, it looks good over your bed."

"But we were going to have a sleepover ..."

"Yeah, I know. It sucks." Alyssa sighed heavily. "My mom said you're welcome to join us."

"What?"

"You know, come to dinner."

"Really?" Madison couldn't believe her ears. Was Alyssa inviting her to have dinner with her TV star mom and a big Hollywood director?

"Not that you'd want to," Alyssa said, shoving her cell phone back into her pack. "It's bound to be boring."

"Are you kidding me? I'd love to go."

"You would?" Alyssa said, looking at Madison with a dubious expression on her face.

"Yeah!" Madison said, jumping to her feet. "Let's go see if my mom will give me permission."

21

crossed lines

"I'm confused," Madison's mom said. "I thought you were having a sleepover."

"We were," Madison said.

"We are," Alyssa chimed in. "We've just made a switch in plans and Madison's going to sleep at my house instead."

Madison blinked. "I am?"

"Yes, of course! Please, Mrs. Stokes," Alyssa said, her hands clasped under her chin, her pleading gaze tilted upward in a very beguiling way.

Hmm ... Madison thought, watching her mother melt, *I should practise that move.*

"Well," her mom said. "I suppose I could put the extra fried chicken in your dad's lunch tomorrow."

"Thank you, Mom!" Madison flung her arms

around her mom's waist and gave her a hug. "You're the best."

"Do you need a ride?" Madison's mom said, switching off the mashed potatoes and starting to remove her apron.

"No, not to worry," Alyssa said hastily. "Max is coming to pick us up."

"Oh, good, I'll wait outside with you and say hello. It will be nice to meet your father."

"Huh?" Madison said, swallowing hard. "Umm ..."

"Great," Alyssa said, grabbing Madison's elbow. "Hey, we'd better go pack you an overnight bag."

"But ..." Madison knew she should say something, but by the time her brain formed a sentence, it was too late. Alyssa had steered her from the room with a cocky "Thanks again, Mrs. Stokes, for letting Madison sleep over tonight!"

The minute they were back in the bedroom, Alyssa's jaunty demeanour dropped away and she was like Eeyore in *Winnie the Pooh* again. "Your mom's making homemade fried chicken?" Alyssa groaned. "I can't believe it—of all the rotten luck. I bet your mom's fried chicken kicks restaurant food's ass."

"Well, I don't know about you," Madison said, throwing her pyjamas and a change of clothes into her backpack. "But eating out in a restaurant is a pretty big deal in our family." She went into the bathroom to get her toothbrush. "What should I do about my mom? She's mixed up about who Max is."

"Don't sweat it," Alyssa said from the bedroom.

"I just ..." Madison began, as she picked up the toothpaste and dental floss and dropped those in her backpack as well. "I don't want to lie to her is all."

"You didn't lie," Alyssa said, poking her head in the bathroom. "You didn't say anything. She assumed."

"Yeah, but ..."

"Look, if you tell her Max is our driver, don't you think she'll wonder? Like, where's my real dad? And who in Rosedale has a chauffeur?"

"I told her you have a housekeeper."

"So, that's different," Alyssa said. "Lots of people have someone clean their house."

"Not really," Madison said.

"Maybe not live-in help, but using a maid service is more common than you think." Alyssa looked at Madison. "Please," she said. "Just leave it. It doesn't hurt anyone, and this way, it doesn't open the door for a million more questions."

Brrring ...

Alyssa checked her cell phone. "Hello? Okay, we'll be right out." She turned the phone off. "Max is here."

Madison could feel Alyssa's expectant gaze on her, but she kept herself busy with the backpack zipper. Her heart felt heavy.

"We've got to get moving," she heard Alyssa say. "My mom has a thing about being punctual."

"Okay." Madison slipped her arms through the straps of her backpack. "Let's go."

22
something's off

"Hello," Madison's mom said, stepping forward to shake Max's hand. "I'm Kathy Stokes. It's so nice to meet you." Madison could see that her mom had run a brush through her hair.

"Nice to make your acvaintance," Max said with a smile, the diamond chip glinting in the overhead streetlight.

Madison saw her mom's gaze take that in and then go right back up to Max's eyes, acting all normal, as though she saw people with diamond chips in their teeth all the time.

"We just love Alyssa," her mom continued, as if she were meeting one of the ladies at church. "She is such a pleasure to have around. You must be so proud of her."

Maximilian blinked, thought that statement

over for a second, and then cleared his throat. "Yes, vee are all proud of her."

"Now, tell me," Madison's mom said. "Did she inherit that quirky sense of humour from you or your wife?"

"Uh ... I'm sorry. I tink—"

Alyssa grabbed Max's arm. "He thinks we have to leave right now, or we're going to be late!" she said, herding him toward the car. "Don't want Mom to get mad now. You know how she is about punctuality."

"All right then." Madison's mom gave a little wave. "It was nice meeting you, Max."

"My pleasure, ma'am," Max said, opening the back door of the car for Alyssa.

"See you tomorrow." As Madison turned to go, her mom swept her into a big hug. "Mom?"

"What's going on?" her mom asked quietly. "Are you okay?"

"Yeah, sure," Madison couldn't meet her eyes. "Of course. Why wouldn't I be?"

"I don't know. Something feels off."

"Maddie, are you coming?" Alyssa called from the back seat.

"I've got to go, Mom. Don't worry, seriously. I'm just going for dinner and a sleepover. Everything's fine."

"All right." Her mom released her reluctantly. "Phone me before you go to sleep, to say good night."

"Okay," Madison said, heading for the car where Max was standing, patiently waiting.

"Promise?" her mom said. She didn't look happy.

"I promise!" And then Max shut the door.

23
dinner out

"Here vee are," Maximilian said, reaching out and swinging the polished brass and glass door wide open. Alyssa and Madison stepped past him and into the restaurant.

A man and woman were in the entryway putting on their coats. The woman was very sleek, with her hair pulled back. She was dressed in a form-fitting little black dress and wore several looping strands of pearls.

Madison looked down at her own clothes. Her shirt was pretty but her jeans were worn and her sneakers were scuffed. Suddenly, she felt nervous.

"Miss Ashton's daughter and her frient," Max told the man at the front, the keys of the town car twirling on his forefinger.

"Very good, sir. This way, please," the mustachioed maître d' replied. His tuxedo-clad arm swept outward, accompanied by a dignified incline of his head.

"See you later, girls. Haf a goot dinner." Maximilian gave a salute as he exited through the gleaming doors and disappeared into the night.

Alyssa followed the maître d', who was gliding through the elegant restaurant. Each table was covered in white linen and decorated with a flickering candle and a slender vase containing a single cream-coloured rose. It was all very fancy, like something out of a movie. Alyssa glanced over her shoulder and gestured to Madison, who hurried to catch up.

The maître d' led the girls toward a discreet booth tucked in an alcove. It had black velvet drapes tied back with thick gold tassels. "Here is your daughter and her friend, Miss Ashton, safe and sound," the maître d' said. Madison thought she saw him smile, but she wasn't sure, because a second later both he and the smile were gone.

"Darling." Alyssa's mother was wearing grey pants and the softest pale peach sweater. She rose from the table and swept Alyssa into a hug, giving her a kiss. "And this must be your friend, Madeline?" She tipped her head to the side slightly, causing the diamond studs in her ears to catch the light and dance and shine like little stars. But more than that, it was the radiance of her smile that nearly knocked Madison off her feet. Jessica Ashton was beautiful, but when she smiled, it seemed to Madison as though an angelic choir had burst into song.

"Her name is *Madison*," she heard Alyssa say, her voice sharp.

"Oh, I'm sorry," Alyssa's mother said, looking a little embarrassed. "I'm terrible with names." She released Alyssa from the hug and stuck out her hand. When Madison stepped close to shake her hand, she could smell the faint scent of honeysuckle. "I'm so pleased to meet you."

"We met once before," Madison said, feeling sort of shy. "You were shooting."

"Yes, that's right." Alyssa's mother turned. "Ted, I'd like you to meet my daughter, Alyssa, and her friend, Madison. Girls, this is Ted Swick, a very talented director and the creator of our show, *Tomorrow's Loss*."

It was the same guy Madison had seen sitting in front of the miniature TV when they were shooting at Shop & Save. "Hey, kids," the director/creator said, getting up slightly from his seat to shake their hands. The pads of his hands were sort of soft. He didn't have rough skin or calluses like Madison's dad.

As they sat down, a waiter materialized. He plucked the white linen napkins off the place settings in front of them and draped them across each of their laps.

"Would the young ladies like something to drink?" he inquired.

"Yeah," Alyssa said with a smirk. "I'll have a bourbon on the rocks."

"Alyssa." Her mom gave her a stern look, but Madison saw a slight upward twitching of her lips.

Mr. Swick laughed, thumping the table with his hand. "What a character!" he hooted. "I bet you're going to be an actress like your mom."

"I'd rather be slowly devoured by rabid rats," Alyssa said, her voice flat. Then she lifted the black leather menu with *Marché* written on it and opened it up to block out his grinning face.

Mr. Swick looked surprised. Alyssa's mother cleared her throat. "Juice okay for you?" she asked Madison.

"Sure," Madison replied. "Juice is fine." The tips of Miss Ashton's ears had gone pink.

"They'll have some juice. Whatever you have," Miss Ashton told the waiter.

"Very good, Miss Ashton," the waiter said, and left.

"So, Jess," the director said, turning his attention back to Miss Ashton. "I thought your scene in the boathouse was wonderful." He draped his arm across the back of her chair, the tips of his fingers brushing her shoulder.

"Ted," Alyssa's mother said softly, shifting her shoulder so his fingers fell away. "Don't."

He pretended she hadn't shrugged him off and kept his arm where it was, but Madison saw a flicker of something cross his face. She wasn't sure what it was: annoyance, perhaps? Anger. Then he smiled and leaned in, reached across Alyssa's mom, and repositioned her fork. "However," he said, his voice soft, "the bedroom scene." He pursed his oversized lips. "It wasn't quite right. You were too ... cold. Frigid, I think is the word. I'll look at the dailies tomorrow, but we'll probably have to reshoot it." He leaned back and replaced his fingers on Miss Ashton's shoulder. She stiffened slightly but didn't shrug him off.

A little while later, Alyssa's mom got up to go to the washroom. When she came back, she needed to talk about something with Alyssa, and so she made Madison change seats with her. It was a little awkward. The director didn't seem too pleased to be sitting next to Madison, but what could he do?

◈

When dinner was over and they came back out through the glass doors, Maximilian was waiting in front of the restaurant with the engine running. A crowd of guys was outside with cameras and they immediately started calling out "Miss Ashton ... Miss Ashton! Over here ... Over here. Smile! Give us a smile!" Their cameras were flashing a mile a minute, which made it hard to see. When Madison had watched this kind of thing on TV, actors arriving for award shows or movie openings, it had always looked so glamorous, the cameras going off, the paparazzi calling their names. But in real life, it was kind of scary; it almost felt like being hunted. Madison's heart was beating fast, her mouth dry—and she wasn't even the one they were taking pictures of.

There was a tug on her hand. "Come on," Alyssa whispered, keeping her head tucked down and turned away from the cameras. Madison tucked her head down too and followed Alyssa as she wove her way around the crowd of photographers and slipped into the back of the car.

"Phew!" Madison said, collapsing on the seat, Maximilian shutting the door behind them. "That was crazy." She tried to sound calm, but she was shaking slightly.

Alyssa shrugged, turning away from the scene,

and stared out through the tinted window as if she could see something in the inky black night.

"How did they know your mom was eating there?"

"No idea," Alyssa said, her voice flat. "They just do. They always do."

Maximilian went back into the crowd, got Alyssa's mom, and helped forge a path for her to the car. He opened the door and Jessica Ashton slipped quickly into the passenger seat, the guys with cameras following her, snapping away.

As Maximilian rounded the car, a rap sounded on Alyssa's mom's window. "Jess ... Jessica!" It was the director. With all the hoopla, Madison had forgotten about him.

"Are we giving *him* a ride?" Alyssa asked.

"God no," Jessica Ashton said. "He brought his car, thank heavens."

Maximilian got in. "Home?" he asked, putting his hand on the gear shift.

The director rapped again and made an unroll-your-window gesture.

Jessica sighed. She held up a finger to Maximilian, then turned and unrolled the window. "Yes?" she said.

Quick as a weasel, the director went in for a kiss, but Alyssa's mom turned her head to the side and caught the kiss on the cheek. Cameras flashing. The director wasn't pleased, but there was nothing he could do about it because before he could make another attempt, Alyssa's mom said, "Night, Ted," and rolled the window back up with a little wave goodbye with her fingers.

It was very smooth how she'd turned her head. Madison filed that tricky move in her memory bank, so that when she was older and had flocks of men wanting to kiss her, she wouldn't have to stand there and let any old guy kiss her on the mouth.

Although if Joey Rodriguez went in for a kiss, Madison thought with a smile, *maybe I'd let him.*

That night as they lay in bed, Alyssa's mom came and tucked them in.

"Night, sweetheart," she said, giving Alyssa a kiss.

"Night, Mom," Alyssa said. Then Miss Ashton leaned over and gave Madison a kiss on the cheek too.

"Good night, Madison."

"Good night, Miss Ashton," Madison said, her hand flying up to her cheek, eyes wide. Jessica Ashton had just kissed her cheek!

Later, with Alyssa asleep beside her, Madison could still feel the imprint where Miss Ashton's lips had touched her cheek. She looked different with her makeup washed off, vulnerable. It seemed to Madison that there was a touch of sadness in Miss Ashton's eyes. But maybe she was just imagining things.

the hollywood insider

"All right, Double Agent O-Three, next task," Madison's dad said through the side of his mouth, sneaking the grocery list from his shirt pocket and taking a furtive peek at it. "Get me a dozen large eggs. I'll do reconnaissance in the baking aisle, see if I can bust some light brown sugar outta da joint. Meet me at the cashier."

"Roger. Copy, over and out," Madison said, her hand cupped around her mouth as if she were speaking into a walkie-talkie. It was a silly game her dad had made up when she was young, pretending to be secret agents. Madison had way outgrown it, but it made him happy. So when there was no one she knew in the store, she'd play along.

"What about me?" Gina said, tugging on his arm. "What's my mission? Huh, Dad? Huh?"

"You're too little," Madison said over her shoulder as she headed down the aisle. "Someone might steal you."

"I'm not too little!" Gina bellowed.

"You need to stick with me, Double Agent O-Four," Madison heard her dad say. "I need you to keep your eyes peeled in case of an ambush."

"Although why anyone would want to steal you," Madison muttered as she loped around the corner, "is beyond me."

It took her all of three seconds to locate the eggs. She arrived at the front where the cashiers were in record time. No sign of her dad and Gina yet, but Madison heard Gina's shrill voice ricocheting out of aisle seven. "Help! Help! A flood of aliens are hot on our heels!" Which was stupid. First of all, they were *secret* agents from the CIA. They did *not* deal with aliens. Second, it was supposed to be a *covert* operation. Covert! That meant no one should *know* what you were doing. You were supposed to act like an invisible ghost, sleuthing along. Not shrieking at the top of your lungs! Embarrassing. *That is it,* Madison thought angrily. *Gina ruined it. I'm done playing this stupid game. Even if quitting hurts Dad's feelings.*

"Yikes!" Gina squealed happily as she and Madison's dad tore around the corner, hunched over the handle of the shopping cart, her dad pulling the plug on a pretend grenade and tossing it over his shoulder.

"Boom!" he said, making a miniature explosion with his hands. Then he smiled, straightened up, dusted off his hands, and ambled toward Madison with an eyebrow cocked. "Mission accomplished?" he asked.

"Yeah, Dad," Madison said, using her normal voice and placing the eggs in the cart. She turned away and pretended to look at the magazines before he could carry on with his goofy game. But out of the corner of her eye, Madison could see him looking at her. He started to open his mouth, but Gina tugged on his arm.

"Can I have some gum, Daddy?"

"No, sweetheart," he said, turning back to Gina and starting to unload the cart.

Madison reached over to help, and that's when she saw it. A big picture of Alyssa's mom on the cover of *The Hollywood Insider* with Ted the director leaning in through the car window, his lips puckered. JESSICA ASHTON'S NEW LOVER! the headline screamed. *Oh my gosh,* Madison thought. *That's horrible. It's just not true. She doesn't even like him.*

She turned away, lifted the milk out of the cart and placed it on the conveyor belt, and then took out the bag of Red Delicious apples and put them on as well. *Stupid magazine.* Madison shook her head. She picked up a jar of baby dill pickles and then, unable to help herself, turned and looked at the magazine again.

Oh no! Madison looked closer. *How could I have missed that?* In the background of the picture, right over Jessica Ashton's shoulder, was a grainy, out-of-focus partial profile of Alyssa and the top of Madison's forehead and part of her left eye.

Madison spun around and looked at her dad. *Did he see? Did he know that was Alyssa and part of his own daughter on that gossip rag?*

No. He was still placidly putting the rest of the groceries on the conveyor belt.

Madison edged over so that her back was covering the magazine. Had anyone else seen it? Could they tell that was her forehead and eye on the cover of *The Hollywood Insider*? What if someone did and made a big noisy fuss? How would she explain this to her parents? Madison hurriedly glanced around. *Oh dear!* A woman at checkout number 3 was looking at the magazine. She *picked* it *up!*

Madison scrunched down a little and held her breath.

The woman flipped the magazine open, and didn't glance over at Madison or anything.

That was a close call.

"You okay?"

Madison jumped, her gaze snapping up to meet her dad's worried eyes.

"Yeah, yeah, I'm fine," she said, pasting a smile on her face. "Just fine."

25
dilemma

Madison felt like a lion in a very small cage as she paced her half of the bedroom, too nervous to settle. In the car on the way home, she hadn't been able to stop thinking about that magazine cover photo. She'd helped unpack the groceries, barely aware of her surroundings. She was still seeing the fake headline, Alyssa's blurry face in profile, and her own eye and forehead, over and over. It was as if the magazine had a grip on her and wouldn't let go, even when Madison tried to force her brain to focus on something else.

She had a slightly sick feeling in the pit of her stomach, like she'd been stuck on a fairground ride that was spinning too fast. No way would they be able to keep Alyssa's mother a secret.

Sure, the picture was blurry, but all it would take was one kid from school standing in the checkout line, looking a little too closely, and the whole thing would blow up. Within an hour everyone in school would know. Sure, some kids would think it was cool, but there were others who'd think Alyssa had tried to put something over on them, and they'd be mad. People like Olivia and Isabelle, for instance. It wouldn't be fun.

Madison needed to do something.

But what?

She strode out of her room. "Dad ..." she called. "Dad?"

No answer.

He wasn't in the kitchen either.

She went out to the garage, and sure enough, there he was, tinkering with the computer he was trying to build from a jumble of parts.

"Can I go over to Grandma and Grandpa's house?"

"It's fine by me if it's okay with them," he said, peering up from his work. "I'll give them a call." He flipped open his cell phone and tapped their name. He didn't have it on speakerphone, but he didn't have to; Madison could hear the phone ring and her grandpa pick up. "Hey, Dad. What are you doing?"

"Nothing much," Madison heard her grandpa say.

"Would it be okay if Madison comes by?"

"That would be great," her grandpa said. "I'll get the Scrabble board ready."

Madison's dad looked at her and raised his eyebrows. Madison nodded, a wave of affection for her dad flooding through her.

"Sure," he said. "Scrabble's great. She's on her way." He flipped the phone shut. "Need a ride, string bean?"

"No thanks. I'll bike."

"Okay then," he said, his attention turning back to the tangle of wires in his hands. "Have fun. Dinner's at six."

Madison strapped on her helmet then wheeled her bike out of the garage and down the drive. She opened the mailbox and looked inside. Nope, nothing from California's Office of Vital Records. Darn.

"Why do you keep checking the mail?"

Madison's head jerked up. Her dad was looking at her with a puzzled expression.

"Oh, no reason," Madison said, feeling her cheeks flush. "See you later." She flung her leg over the crossbar, jammed her foot on the pedal, and pushed off before her dad could ask her more questions. She rose out of her bike seat and pedalled hard. She needed to put some distance between her and her lies. She wasn't sure what she was going to say to her grandpa. She just knew she needed to get advice from someone. And her grandpa was the wisest person she knew.

26
grandpa's words

Madison shuffled the Scrabble tiles on her rack. Her letters were pretty good; it was her brain that wasn't cooperating. She shuffled them again.

"Are you all right?" her grandpa asked.

Madison looked up. He wasn't in his usual Scrabble-playing position, hunched over his tiles, figuring out his next move. He was sitting back in his armchair, studying her over the top of his bifocals.

She opened her mouth to say sure, but she couldn't. It was as if her mouth refused to lie again. Madison stared back down at her tiles, miserable. She pretended to shuffle them, but the move was pointless. She couldn't see the letters because her eyes were suddenly blurry.

Her grandpa leaned forward, slid his tiles

and the board to the side, and placed his warm, weathered hand on hers. "What's up, buttercup?" he asked. His gruff voice was gentle.

"I don't know what to do, Grandpa," Madison blurted out. "I'm in a mess and I don't know how to untangle it. My friend asked me to keep a secret, and I promised I would. I pinky-swore. And it didn't seem like a big deal at the time, but now ..." She shook her head. "I didn't know that to keep my promise to her, I was going to have to lie to my mom and dad."

Madison's grandpa let out a long, low whistle. "That *is* serious," he said. "I can see why you're upset."

"And you, Grandpa." Madison made herself look up at him, square in the face, even though she couldn't hide the hot tears that were falling. "I even lied to you."

But he didn't turn away in anger or disgust. He just nodded his head and scrubbed his bristly chin with his hand, absorbing what she'd said. "Are you sorry?" he asked.

"Awfully sorry," Madison said, nodding, warm wet salt in her mouth.

"Then I forgive you," her grandpa replied. "And I'm sure your mom and dad will too."

"Do you think?"

"I *know*." The way he said it lightened her heart. "It sounds," he continued, "like a complicated situation."

"It is," Madison said. "And I don't want to keep lying, but I don't want to break my promise, either."

"Follow your gut, Madison," her grandpa said. "Listen to your heart. It won't lead you astray. When you look inside, deep down in your belly, you'll know what to do."

27
a decision

Madison stared down at her dinner plate. It was her favourite meal of all time—lasagna and garlic bread, with its perfect combination of soft, buttery inside and crisp, chewy crust to mop up leftover lasagna sauce or gobble down by itself—and she couldn't eat a bite. Her throat felt constricted.

"Madison, honey, why aren't you eating?" Her mom had a slight furrow on her brow.

"I'm not hungry."

"You're always hungry," her mom said, shaking her head. "Especially when it's lasagna."

"Too many cookies and cashews," her dad said with a wink.

"I don't think so, Robert. She looks tuckered out." Her mom reached over and placed the back of her hand against Madison's forehead. "No fever. Is your throat sore? Do you have a headache?"

"No, Mom, I just——"

"*I'm* eating," Gina piped up. "Look at me. I'm eating good."

"Shut up," Madison muttered.

"Madison," her mom said. "We do not say 'shut up' in this family. It's rude. Apologize to your sister."

"Sorry."

"It's okay," Gina said, smiling magnanimously. "And I forgive you for the two shut ups last night as well."

Little brat. The moment that thought flew out of her brain, Madison felt ashamed. It was as if she'd spent her life thinking she was one kind of person, only to look in the mirror and find someone totally different staring back at her. When had she started telling her little sister to shut up all the time? She never used to do that. How had she gotten to be such a grump? Mean to her sister, lying to her dad, her mom, her grandpa, all because of trying to keep Alyssa's secret. And now her mother was worried she was sick.

"Come to think of it," her dad said, "she *was* awfully quiet on the way home from the store this afternoon."

"You look a little pale, Maddie. You'd better

go lie down. I'll heat you up a can of soup." Her mother rose from the table and went to the cupboard.

"Mom, really, I'm fine."

"I hope you aren't coming down with that nasty stomach flu going around. Let's see," her mom said, peering into the cupboard. "We have turkey rice or chicken noodle. Which one will it be, sweetheart?"

"I'm *not* hungry!"

"No need to be snippy, young lady," her dad interjected. "Your mother is just trying to help."

Madison looked from her dad's stern face to her mom's anxious one. There was no way out of this. "Fine," she said and sighed. "Chicken noodle, please. Thanks, Mom." She pushed back from the table and started to pick up her plate.

"Maddie, don't worry about that, sweetie," her mom said, twisting the can-opener knob. "I'll take care of it later. You go get in your pyjamas. I'll bring your soup when it's warm."

Madison nodded, feeling like an even worse fake than she did before. "Thank you, Mom."

By the time she'd changed into her pyjamas and gotten into bed, Madison had made a decision. She was going to talk to Alyssa tomorrow and get out of the pinky-swear. She couldn't go on like this. Alyssa would understand.

28
the fight

"What?" Alyssa thrust her head forward, eyes narrowed. "Please tell me you're joking."

"I ... It's just ..." Madison stammered. The look on Alyssa's face was disbelief, anger, and fear, all mixed up. "I'm sorry, Alyssa, it's just too hard. I ... I can't keep on lying to ..." Madison swallowed hard. The words weren't coming out right. "Lying to ..."

Alyssa took a step back, eyes widening. "Oh my god," she said slowly. "You *aren't* joking, are you?" She shook her head slowly. "I trusted you. I thought you were different. What an idiot I am."

"No, you don't understand, *The Hollywood Insider*—"

"*The Hollywood Insider*? What? You think just because you've *met* my mom, had dinner with her *once*, that that makes you an expert, a reliable source? Boy, those tabloids are scraping the bottom of the barrel by coming to you, because you, my dear, know *nothing*!"

"Alyssa," Madison said, trying to keep her voice quiet, even though they were out in the far corner of left field and no one was within hearing range. It was drizzling out, so most of the kids had stayed inside for lunch. "If you would just let me explain—"

"Oh believe me, darling." Alyssa's eyes were angry slits, her voice dripping with hostility. "I understand totally. *It's too hard!*" she mimicked. "What's it been, three *whole* weeks of keeping my secret? Wow, that *is* stamina! What a good friend you are. Bravo." She clapped her hands, a bitter sneer on her face. Alyssa's stare swept up and down Madison like a blowtorch. "How much did the *Insider* offer you and your grubby little family in your rinky-dinky house? God knows, I'm sure you could use the money."

"You have no right." It felt as though Alyssa had just reached out and slapped her. Madison didn't want to sell stories to tabloids. How could Alyssa even think that about her? She just didn't want to lie to her family anymore. What kind of friend would insist on that? "At least," she choked out, her vision blurry with angry tears, "at least I *have* a family, a nice one, unlike you with your big rented house and your hired help. And guess what else, Miss Fancy-Pants. I wouldn't trade lives with you for a million dollars!"

The girls stared at each other, breathing hard. "By the way," Alyssa spat out, her face cold, fists clenched. "I don't release you. The pinky-swear stands. And if you break it, a black curse will be on the heads of you and your loved ones forever-more." And the way Alyssa said it, with such venom, as if she were taking an oath, caused a shudder to run through Madison. Because in that moment, with the wind whipping about and Alyssa's hair hanging in wet strands around her twisted, angry face, she looked almost like a witch casting a spell.

Madison's heart was pounding hard in her temples and throat. "I hate you." Madison thought she had yelled it, but it came out almost a whisper that hovered in the air for a moment before it landed and caused the remaining blood to drain from Alyssa's face.

Then Madison turned and walked stiff-backed toward the school, leaving her ex–best friend standing in the field.

The drizzle had now turned into a torrential downpour, with sheets of icy rain blowing across the field and soaking through her jacket and jeans. But Madison didn't run. Normally, getting drenched at lunch hour was not desirable since the afternoon would be spent in wet clothes, but in this instance, Madison was grateful for the camouflage. Rivulets of rain mingled with the angry tears streaming down her face, leaking into her mouth, filling it with the bitter taste of salt and words that wanted to come out. The real ones she had planned on saying that were still wedged in her throat, jammed down, unspoken, aborted. And now it was too late to talk, too late to explain. Everything was ruined.

29
the creature

The door was heavier than usual with the wind blowing against it, the metal handle cold and slippery in her wet hand. Madison stepped into the hall, the door thumping shut behind her. "Whoohoo," she heard a boy exclaim. She kept her head tucked down, her hair falling forward and shielding her face. She'd know that voice blindfolded. It was stupid Joey Rodriguez.

"Figures," she muttered.

"Oh my god! What *is* it?" Joey wailed, recoiling in horror.

"Help," Dylan shrieked, flinging an arm across his eyes, as if the sight of her was terrifying. "It's the Creature from the Black Lagoon!" And yes, she was soggy and was leaving a trail of water behind her, but still, did they have to make such a big deal about it?

"Ahhh ... Help!" Two other boys, Brian and Tom, ran screaming down the hall, arms waving like windmills.

Normally Madison would have laughed and tossed a smart-aleck comment their way, but not today. She sped up her steps.

"Please." Joey threw himself on his knees in front of her, his hands clasped together in prayer. "Don't kill meeeee!"

"Go away," she forced out through clenched teeth, keeping her head turned away from him.

"Yikes!" Joey fell backward and started scrabbling crablike down the hall in front of her, pretending he was trying to escape. "The monster sp-sp-speaks."

"Get ... lost." Madison whirled her face around to glare at him. "I mean it!" she said, kicking out with her foot. She didn't intend to make contact with his leg, but Joey didn't try to get out of the way. It was as if he was frozen for a second, staring up at her face. "What are you looking at?" she said, but the second the words left her mouth, she knew. He could see her swollen, red-rimmed eyes. She could tell by his expression that he knew she'd been crying. Madison quickly turned her face back toward the wall and stepped over his sprawled body, her shoulders braced for the ridicule that was sure to follow.

She could still hear Dylan thumping around the hall on stiff legs, arms outstretched. "The creature ... the creature ..." he groaned in a gloomy monotone, but oddly enough, there was no laughter or comment from Joey.

The girls' bathroom was ahead on the left. Madison lunged for the door and slipped inside. It was empty, thank god. She grabbed a handful of paper towels and darted into an empty stall, locking the door behind her.

She looked at the wad of towels in her hand. She was shaking and her legs were suddenly wobbly, as if they might give way. She sat down, her head sinking into her hands, her mind spinning, trying to make sense of what had happened. Somehow the conversation with Alyssa had veered off track like a runaway train and she'd gotten tangled up in Alyssa's misconceptions about the situation. Instead of explaining, Madison had panicked and flailed out. *I hate you ...* The echo of those words reverberated around the empty bathroom, bouncing off the walls, along with the memory of the look on Alyssa's face. *I hate you ...* Why had she said that to her friend? Madison's eyes welled up. "Stop it," she whispered, shaking her head angrily. *Lunch is going to be over soon and you don't want to go back to class looking like a crybaby.*

She pressed the palms of her hands against her eyes. Alyssa had been wrong too, Madison reminded herself. She'd said mean things about Madison's family and their home.

At least I have a family, she heard her own voice mocking. *A nice one.* Oh, she'd been horrible. She'd hit below the belt. Alyssa was never going to forgive her. And with that thought, another wave of sadness came.

Enough, she told herself. She wiped her face and then rubbed the paper towels in her hair, trying to soak up the rain.

The jarring lunch bell startled her for a second. "Great," she said. She stood up and reluctantly unlocked the door. As the stall door swung open, she caught sight of her face in the mirror. Yuck. It was red and blotchy. She went to the sink and splashed some cold water on her eyes, but it didn't help. She still looked lousy. She dried her face, dropped the towel in the garbage, squared her shoulders, took a deep breath, and exited the bathroom.

As Madison made her way through the crowded hall to her classroom, she could feel her face heat up. What was she going to do when she saw Alyssa? Maybe she should pretend nothing had happened, that neither of them had said those angry words. But what if she smiled and said hi and Alyssa turned away without speaking, or yelled something mean? Madison paused outside her classroom, battling a wave of jangly nerves. She took another deep breath, and on the exhale, forced herself to walk through the doorway.

I won't look at her side of the room, she decided, but she hadn't taken more than five steps before her gaze found its way to Alyssa's desk.

Her seat was empty.

Madison's heart started to pound fast. She sank into her own seat slowly. *Where was she? Why wasn't she here?*

Ms. Elliot entered the room, slightly breathless. "Sorry, I got a little held up in the staff room," she said, using her foot to push the classroom door shut. She was carrying a stack of handouts and the red, apple-shaped coffee mug that was never far from her grasp.

Madison watched as the door clicked shut. Alyssa must be here. Maybe she'd been putting her jacket in her cubby when Madison first looked over. She bent over and pretended to be looking for something in her desk, using the movement to glance around the room again. No Alyssa.

"Take one and pass it back," Ms. Elliot said, plopping some of the handouts on the first desk in every row.

Was she still outside? Maybe she tripped and twisted her ankle and was lying out on the field in the rain. Madison looked out the window anxiously. But she couldn't see the field from this side of the building. Just a bit of yard, a portion of the jungle gym, and the empty swings swaying in the wind as though ghost children were sitting in them and rocking gently, dragging their feet.

Bruised, swollen clouds were lying low in the sky, making everything dark. The rain was splattering against the classroom windows, so heavily that Madison almost didn't see the black town car gliding slowly down the road.

What was that? It looked for a moment as if the big Garry oak tree had started to move, and then Madison saw it: the flash of purple as a dark-silhouetted wraith of a girl sprinted from behind the tree, climbed over the chain-link fence, and slipped into the waiting car.

"Madison," Sarah said, twisting in her desk and holding out the worksheets. "Come on."

Madison took the sheets from Sarah, put one on her desk, and handed the rest to Isabelle behind her. *Reading Comprehension: Winter* was written at the top of the page.

She glanced back out the window. The town car was gone. It almost felt as though she'd imagined it. *Did Alyssa have permission to leave? Did she sign out at the principal's office? What did she tell them? Had she been crying too?*

Madison's throat got that achy-sore tightness of emotions suppressed. She made herself focus on the paper in front of her. *Cold winter temperatures are caused by the tilting of the Earth. When Earth's northern hemisphere is tilted away from the sun ...*

That's how she felt. Tilted away from the sun.

30
lost

On the bike ride home from school, Madison replayed the fight over and over in her head. Yeah, she'd said some mean things, but Alyssa had too! Like calling Madison's family grubby and their house rinky-dinky. "Well, ex*cuse* me," Madison sneered under her breath, making a right on her street and not even bothering to duck her shoulders into her jean jacket anymore. It was pointless. The rain was coming down in sheets. She was soaked right through to her underwear. "I'm so sorry that I don't have a fancy stick-up-the-butt housekeeper and chauffeur and a lah-di-dah movie-star mother."

She turned into her driveway, the bike skidding out slightly on the wet asphalt. She didn't even bother checking the mailbox. Who cared who Alyssa's stinky father was? She rode right up to the garage, dismounted, and wheeled her bike in. *Alyssa was a stupid friend anyway. What kind of friend won't even let you talk? Wants to make you lie to everyone, lie to your family? That's not a friend!*

Madison stalked through the kitchen and down the hall.

"Madison," her dad called. "You're leaving a soppy mess."

"I'll get it in a minute!" she yelled, slamming into her bedroom, storming over to the painting above her bed, and yanking it off the wall.

Then she marched down into the basement and put the painting next to the box of giveaway stuff. "There," she said, dusting off her hands. "Good riddance." And it felt good.

She returned to her room. It was weird how she'd gotten so used to seeing Alyssa's painting there. The wall above her bed seemed blank, unfinished. "What*ever*," Madison said.

She got changed into dry clothes and then got the mop out of the kitchen cupboard and wiped up the trail of water she had tracked through the house.

◈

That night, Madison woke. She wasn't sure what had made her wake up, but there she was, at two forty-five in the morning, staring at the wall where Alyssa's painting had been. Sorrow about the whole fight, the whole misunderstanding, was sitting like a weight on her chest.

She got out of bed, the floor cold under her feet, and tiptoed down to the basement, heart racing like crazy because the basement was a little scary at night. She grabbed the painting and hurried back to her bedroom, climbed up on her bed, and replaced it on the wall.

It fit there. It was like it belonged.

Madison got back into bed and snuggled under the covers. They were still warm. *Tomorrow,* she thought right before she drifted off to sleep, *I'll talk to her tomorrow and try to sort this whole thing out.*

31
lunch

It was overcast, but the rain had stopped and so lunch was outside. Madison stood on the bottom step that led from the school down to the patio. She felt awkward standing there, not knowing where to sit, her lunch bag in her hand. It had been a week since their big fight and Alyssa still hadn't come back to school. It was bad enough during class time with her empty desk sitting there, but lunchtime and recess were the hardest.

"I wish she'd never come," Madison muttered. At least before Alyssa moved to Rosedale, Madison had friends, people to eat lunch with. But now she had no one.

The only spot left was at one of the grey metal tables where Isabelle and Olivia were chatting away. When Madison sat down, Isabelle turned her back like she had cooties or something and whispered to Olivia behind her hand. Both of them giggled. Madison pretended she didn't care. She could feel the cold metal damp of the bench through her jeans.

Olivia peeled the cover back from her lunch pack. "Yum," she said. "Pizza."

Madison opened her lunch box and removed her egg salad sandwich from its Tupperware container.

"Ew ..." Isabelle said, wrinkling her nose and waving her hand in front of her face. "Something stinks."

Like she could even smell it from that far away. "Shut up," Madison said, taking a bite.

"You should get your mom to buy you Lunchables," Olivia said, carefully spreading a layer of pizza sauce on her cracker and then sprinkling some mozzarella cheese on top. "They're really tasty."

Was Olivia talking to her? Must be, since both Olivia and Isabelle had pizza Lunchables. *Did they call each other up the night before and decide to be twins for lunch?* she wondered. Just imagining that scintillating conversation made Madison grin.

"Don't talk to her," Isabelle said, poking Olivia with her elbow. "We're not her friend anymore."

"No, we're *her* friend," Olivia said, "just not *Alyssa's*."

"Whatever," Madison said with a shrug. It was stupid how they'd rejected Alyssa right off the bat, without even trying to get to know her. How had she ever been friends with people like that? Guess she'd never noticed how narrow-minded they were.

Isabelle broke off a piece of her miniature pizza and popped it in her mouth. The tangy pizza sauce smelled good.

Madison took a bite of her egg salad sandwich. Her teeth found a little piece of eggshell, but she didn't spit it out. No way would she give Olivia and Isabelle another reason to act superior. Just because their families could afford to waste money on fancy pre-made lunches didn't make them better than her.

She took another bite. Isabelle was right. Egg salad sandwiches *were* a little smelly.

"Hey, by the way, where *is* Alyssa?" Isabelle asked.

Madison shrugged. "Why are you asking me? I'm not her keeper."

"I don't know. I figured you were friends." Isabelle exchanged a look with Olivia.

"Not really," Madison said. She could feel her face grow hot. She lifted up the top layer of bread and looked inside her sandwich as though she was interested in something in there.

"They had a fight," Olivia said, taking another bite, watching Madison closely over the top of her pizza.

"I don't know what you're talking about."

"Give it up, Maddie," Olivia said, the expression in her eyes a mix of smug and sad. "We saw the two of you outside screaming at each other last week. And then you come back, your face all red, and Alyssa disappears."

"If that's not a fight," Isabelle added, "I don't know what is."

"Huh," Madison said, getting to her feet, struggling to hide how this conversation was making her feel. "There's a bit of shell in here. Mom must have let Gina help her peel the eggs." She walked over to the garbage can and threw the sandwich in.

"How long has she been away?" Olivia asked.

Madison didn't turn around. "A week," she heard herself say.

"Thursday is Halloween, and if she's still sick, she's going to miss all the fun," Isabelle said.

Olivia took a delicate bite of her pizza and dabbed her mouth with a napkin. "Maybe she's got that swine flu."

"Eew!" Isabelle squealed. "I bet she does.

Brought the germs from wherever it is she's from. Where exactly in L.A. did she live?"

Olivia laughed. "Probably the slums."

No, Malibu, Madison thought, but she didn't say it, just shrugged. "I don't know. What difference does it make?" She returned to the table and picked up her lunch bag. "See you guys later."

"Where are you going?" Olivia asked.

"Library. I didn't finish up my homework last night, so I figure I'd better do it now."

The library was quiet and pretty empty. There were a couple of kids on the computers. Sarah from her class was curled up in an armchair in the corner with her nose tucked in a book.

Madison sat at a cubby so that no one would talk to her. She needed to think, clear her mind. Olivia was just being mean. Alyssa wasn't sick. She didn't have swine flu. At least, Madison didn't think she did. That would be horrible. Perfectly healthy people *died* from swine flu. Here one day, gone the next. *You're being ridiculous,* she told herself. *Your imagination is running rampant. Leave it alone. Do your homework.*

Madison opened her math workbook to page forty-eight and stared at it, but she wasn't seeing the numbers. *What if Lyssa really is sick?* the voice in her head whispered. *Maybe she needs you.*

32
crossed connections

Instead of turning right out of the schoolyard, Madison had turned left. She'd been biking now for quite some time. Her legs were sore and the pale light of the cloud-smeared sun was just starting to disappear behind the trees. Alyssa's home hadn't seemed that far away in the car with Maximilian driving. She hadn't even hit Willows Beach yet. *Maybe I took a wrong turn,* Madison thought, but she kept on pedalling.

What was I thinking? This is what Mom's always getting upset about, me flying off to do something without figuring out a plan. It was going to be dark soon, and what was she going to do then? It was illegal to ride a bike at night without a headlight.

Oh, thank heavens! She was on the right track. There was Willows Beach up on the right. It was deserted. The wind tumbled an empty plastic bag across the sand until it got caught up around the leg of an old brown picnic table.

Madison pedalled on. Her gaze scanned the fancy driveways on the right, with their tall, lush hedges, ornate fences, and granite stone walls. *Was that one it?* Madison slowed to a halt. No, it was a different gate. This one was wrought iron, and Alyssa's house had a wooden gate with black hinges.

The sun had totally disappeared behind the trees now and the temperature seemed to drop a couple of degrees. Madison shivered. *I should have used the school office phone to call home and let Dad know I was going to be late. He's going to be ticked off.* Even though she was sweating from biking so far, the cold was starting to penetrate. Madison zipped her jacket up a bit higher and pushed off again. Her legs were tired.

A few more blocks and there it was, Alyssa's drive. Madison was sure of it. The gate was closed. Now what? She didn't have that little remote gate opener that Max had in his jacket pocket. She dropped her bike on the ground and tried to scale the wall, but it was too high, and even standing on her tippytoes, her fingers couldn't get a grip on the top.

"Alyssa!" Madison yelled, although she knew it was pointless. The house was too far from the gate for Alyssa to hear. But maybe she was walking outside and the wind would carry Madison's voice to her. "Hey, Lyssa! It's me, Madison!" She waited, listening hard.

Nothing.

It was getting dark fast. She was going to be in big trouble. Grounded for sure. "Alyssa!"

Nothing.

What a waste of time. What was she hoping to achieve? And for all she knew, Alyssa could be standing on the other side of the wall, listening to Madison and laughing. She shouldn't have come.

Wait a minute. There was a little voice box attached to a metal pole by the gate. Madison ran over.

It had a keypad with numbers on it and a black button. Madison pressed the button. *Rrring ... rrring ...*

Her heart was pounding. If she got Alyssa, what was she going to say? She hadn't thought that far ahead.

Rrring ... rrring ...

Suddenly she had the impulse to run away.

Rrring ... rrring ...

There was the sound of the phone being picked up. Madison's mouth was dry.

"Hola?"

Oh darn! What was Alyssa's housekeeper's name?
She knew it. It was hovering just past the tip of
her tongue.

"Hola? Hola?"

"Um ... hello. This is Madison. I don't know
if you remember me, but I'm a friend of Alyssa's
from school."

"Perdón? No entiendo lo que usted dice." Oh no!
Alyssa's housekeeper speaks Spanish. Madison had
forgotten about that.

"Um ... I'm sorry, I ... uh ..." Madison could
feel her face turn red. This was so awkward.
"Could you please tell Alyssa that I'm at the gate
and would like to talk with her, if it's possible? I
mean if she's not sick in bed or something?"

*"Por favor hable más despacio, tal vez puedo
entenderlo."*

"What?" Madison was starting to feel sweaty.
"Oh dear." This was really embarrassing. "I'm
sorry I bothered you. I'm not trying to be rude
or anything. I just don't understand what you're
saying."

*"Le diré lo que, usted espera ahí mismo. Ella está
en su dormitorio. Iré la consiguen y la rebajan."*

Maybe, Madison suddenly thought, *Alyssa's
housekeeper could understand English, even though she
couldn't speak it.* It was a long shot. Madison took
a deep breath and plunged in, speaking slowly. "I

was worrying about Alyssa, that maybe she was sick or something and needed me to bring her homework so she won't get behind."

There was no answer.

"Also," Madison continued, feeling the embarrassed heat rising in her face, "I wanted to remind her that Thursday is Halloween, and I hope she's better by then. If she is, could you let her know that I'm still going to be a broken dead doll, and I hope she is too?"

Alyssa's housekeeper still didn't respond. This was pointless. The gate remained firmly shut, and sometime in the last ten minutes, the sky had gone from dusk to dark. It had also started to sprinkle. Madison sighed. "I'm sorry," she said. "I better get home. Thank you for talking with me. Bye."

She picked up her bike off the ground, started to hoist her leg over, and then remembered she couldn't ride without a headlight. She sighed again.

It was going to be a long walk home.

33
willows beach

By the time Madison reached Willows Beach, the light sprinkle had turned into a hard-driving rain. She was cold. She was wet. She was hungry. A large blister was forming on her left heel. "Why," she muttered for the umpteenth time. "*Why* won't my parents let me have a cell phone?" She flicked a strand of wet hair out of her face, and that's when she saw the old pay phone on the side of the snack shack, its receiver dangling by the cord.

Did it work?

She hobbled over, leaned her bike against the building, hung up the phone, and then lifted it off its cradle again.

Yes!

She tapped in her home phone number collect. The electronic operator came on and asked her to say her name, then put her on hold.

The phone had barely started its first ring when it was snatched up. "Hello?" It was her dad.

"Would you accept a collect call from Madison?" the electronic voice asked him.

"God, yes." He didn't sound good. The operator completed the call.

"Dad?" Madison said. "Are you okay?"

"Madison! Where the *hell* are you?" he bellowed. "You were supposed to come straight home to babysit Gina. I had to cancel a job interview. Couldn't take her with me. Not exactly conducive interviewing circumstances, especially since I was worried out of my goddamned mind about you!"

Uh-oh … Her dad *never* swore.

"Sorry … I forgot …"

"Forgot? You forgot? I've been sick with worry. Where are you?"

"I … I'm at Willows Beach." Her voice coming out small. "I was wondering if you would pick me up?"

"Willows Beach? What in god's name are you doing there? Please, Maddie-girl, tell me you're all right." He sounded like he was choking back tears. And just the thought of her dad crying made her eyes fill up as well.

"Yeah, Dad, I'm fine. I just—"

"Oh, thank god in heaven! I'll be right there. Don't move. Ten minutes tops."

Madison's dad hung up.

Madison slowly replaced the receiver. Her dad was really upset. She wrapped her arms tightly around her torso to try to contain the shivering, but it didn't help much. The icy rain had already penetrated to the marrow of her bones. Her breath was coming out in puffs of steam. She stomped her feet to try to warm them, her sneakers making wet squishing sounds on the pavement that surrounded the snack shack.

As she waited, Madison's thoughts turned back to Alyssa's house. Did the housekeeper understand what Madison had been saying? Had Alyssa told her not to let her in?

The old blue family station wagon screeched to a shuddering halt. Madison's dad leapt out of the driver's seat, slammed the door, and started across the grass at a brisk jog. The next thing Madison knew he had her clutched in a fierce bear hug.

"Don't you *ever*," he said, pulling back and giving her a shake, his hands gripping her shoulders, "*ever* scare me like that again. Do you hear me?" And of course she could hear him because he was yelling his head off. "It is *not* allowed! If you're going to be late, if you make other plans, you *must* call." And before she could respond, he'd pulled her back against his chest in a smothering hug. She could hear the thump of his heart. "Promise me."

"I promise," Madison said, and she meant it, too.

34
broken dolls

It had been ten days since the fight. Alyssa's birth certificate still hadn't come in the mail. Madison checked several times a day. There was no sign of Alyssa, either. And last night at dinner, Madison's dad commented on the fact that Alyssa hadn't been around. Made a joke about it, saying the food bill was showing a marked improvement. He stopped teasing, though, when he noticed Madison wasn't laughing.

"What is it, poppet?" he'd asked. Madison had wanted to tell him everything, get his advice and her mom's, too. But instead she got up from the table, went to the stove, and dropped another dollop of mashed potatoes on her plate, blinking back the sudden heat in her eyes.

A week and a half. It felt like an eternity. Madison stared at her reflection in the bathroom mirror. Her Halloween costume looked good, weird and scary. She pulled another few strands of hair from her braids to hang in disarray around her face. It had been a good touch making the part crooked.

Her gaze travelled down to the rest of her outfit. She'd squeezed into one of Gina's dresses, and was wearing red-and-white striped tights and her dad's boxer shorts with the red hearts. Madison had cajoled her mom into sewing elastic around the bottom of the legs so they looked like short bloomers. Then, topping it all off, she had a white flounced apron on which she had drawn a red heart and written in her best cursive, *I love you*.

Her mind flashed to Alyssa. Was she going to be at school today? If she did come, would she be a broken dead doll like they'd planned back when they were friends? Just thinking about it made Madison feel all constricted in her throat again.

She rolled her shoulders, shook the tension from her arms, and focused back on the mirror. Greyish-white makeup covered her face, neck, and hands. She'd drawn matching red circles on each cheek, a red dot on her nose, and small, pursed red lips in the centre of her blanked-out mouth. Then in black she'd drawn long dark eyelashes.

Did Alyssa's housekeeper tell her that Madison had been by? Maybe Alyssa had been sitting right there in the kitchen having a snack and had heard the whole thing and was laughing behind her hand. That would suck, and if she *had* done that, it would be over for good, whether Alyssa wanted to be friends again or not.

Madison's stomach hurt. She reached up and tweaked the wrinkled red bow in her hair.

Besides, she thought, *maybe Alyssa will show up today and wear her broken dead doll outfit, too*. But how would Madison know if that was a sign she still wanted to be friends? Maybe Alyssa's house-keeper hadn't been able to give her Madison's message.

Just thinking about it made Madison feel jittery and scared and kind of hopeful inside.

Her dad poked his head in the bathroom. "Whoa, awesome outfit. You look good, honey."

"Thanks, Dad," Madison said. He hadn't stayed upset. Hadn't grounded her or anything, just hugged her a lot and sat both her and Gina down to clarify the rules for when one *has* to call home. Explained that going for a long impromptu bike ride to Willows Beach after school *was* one of those times. Her dad was like that, he didn't hold a grudge, but still, she felt terrible about scaring him so badly and messing up his interview. The next day he'd called and tried to reschedule, but the job had already been filled.

"Are you ready for me to work my magic?" he asked.

Madison nodded.

"Excellent." He bounded into the bathroom with the bag of Halloween special-effects makeup he'd saved up over the years. "All right." He dumped the contents on the counter and stretched out his arms and hands as though he was preparing for surgery. "Let's rock and roll."

He carefully added a scar with stitches that was oozing blood across her forehead and into her hairline, matting her hair around it with blood. Then he stood back and admired his handiwork, squinting slightly. "Perfect," he said. "And now ..." He dabbed some makeup around her left eye, rubbed a little, dabbed a bit more. When he stepped back, Madison had a black eye.

"That looks great, Dad," she said with a shiver, examining the purplish-black bruise.

"Wait!" He stepped forward and added a tinge of yellow to the bruise and a bit of red around the rim of her eye. "There we go. That's more like it."

He added some dirt smears on her apron and then stood back and splattered some fake blood on her. He was flinging his arms around like a mad scientist. Madison didn't want to ruin his fun, so she didn't point out that he was splattering fake blood on the wall and sink as well.

"This is great!" he crowed. "Now, tilt your head a little." The skin on his palm felt warm and dry against her cheek. "Perfect," he grinned. "Open your eyes wide. Yikes!" he yelped. "You're giving me the shivers." He took her hand. "All right, pumpkin," he said. "Let's go scare the bejesus out of your mom and little sister."

Madison walked down the hall, her head tilted to the side, keeping her movements sort of stiff, jerky, and floppy all at once, like she was partially defrosted and trying to learn how to move her limbs again.

"Fantastic," her dad cackled.

Her mom was not so impressed. "Oh, Robert," she sighed when she caught sight of Madison. "Really, don't you think that's a little gruesome for fifth grade?"

"How can you say that?" he protested. "It is art. It is inspired. It is brilliant!"

"How can I *say* that? I wonder." She glanced behind her meaningfully. Only Gina's hands, desperately clutching their mom's skirt, and the tips of her sparkly fairy wings were visible.

"Make it go away ..." Gina wailed.

"Don't be such a baby," Madison replied, feeling quite smug.

Gina's head poked out from behind their mom, her eyes wide, lower lip trembling. "Ma ... Madison?"

"Yes," Madison said in her normal voice, and then lurched her head to the side and started her broken-doll walk toward her sister. "Let me ..." she began in a creepy, high-pitched monotone, "give ... you ... a ... hug."

"Noooo!" Gina shrieked, diving behind their mom again. "Mommy, save me."

"Madison Harriet Stokes, you smarten up right now," her mom snapped.

"Sorry, Mom," Madison said, but she wasn't. The look of terror on Gina's face had been very satisfying.

Gina refused to walk to school with Madison, so their mom had to drop her little sister off on the way to work. She offered Madison a lift too, but Madison wanted to ride her bike to help burn off some of her nervous energy. The rain held off, which was good. It would have sucked to arrive with her makeup all smeared and running down her face.

She steered her bike right into an open slot and unlooped her bike lock from the back of her seat.

"Whoa, great costume, Mad-one."

Madison looked over. It was Joey. She'd been avoiding him ever since the incident in the hall. "Get lost," she muttered, snapping her bike lock shut and heading toward the school, but that didn't deter Joey. He locked up his bike and jogged a couple of steps until he caught up with her. She wanted to run, but that would look stupid, so she just kept walking as if he wasn't there.

"No, I mean it," he replied. "It's really ... um ... interesting. What are you supposed to be?"

Madison glanced at him, braced for the wisecrack. It didn't come.

"I'm a broken dead doll," she finally answered.

"Duh." He thunked his palm against his forehead. "I don't know why I didn't guess that. It's exactly what you look like. The best costume ever. You look really creepy. In a good way," he added hastily, throwing his hands up as if to say, Don't hit me. Which made Madison laugh, even though she was nervous about whether Alyssa would show. Joey laughed too. He had a nice smile, and a sprinkle of cinnamon-coloured freckles across the bridge of his nose. She'd never noticed that before.

"Guess what I am?" he asked, posing like a store mannequin. It looked funny to see him act so debonair, especially since he was wearing an oversized pair of green fishing waders with suspenders and a forest-green sweater, a strand of tiny light bulbs wrapped all around him. "Wait!" Joey grabbed the end of the cord that was dangling from a belt cinched to his waist and plugged it into a pouch on his side. Suddenly the strand lit up in little multicoloured lights. "What do you think?"

"Wow!" Madison laughed, clapping her hands. "Fantastic."

"What am I?" he asked.

"I don't know, but it's ingenious!"

"I'm a Christmas tree," he said, bumping her with his shoulder.

Madison felt warm, her face flushed. "Oh, yes, of course," she replied, bumping him back like it was no big deal. "How did you make the lights work?"

"Oh, me and my dad rigged it up in his workshop. See in here." He unsnapped the top of the pouch and flipped it back, acting all modest and nonchalant, but Madison could tell he was proud. "It's a battery pack." He struck a muscle-man pose. "I'm packing my own power."

"Very cool." They smiled at each other. He had golden flecks mixed in with the brown in his eyes.

"Hey, look, I'm sorry about the other day," Joey said, suddenly serious. "In the hall. We were just teasing. I didn't know you'd been …"

"It's okay." Madison shrugged. She felt uncomfortable, and wished he hadn't brought it up.

"Hey, Joey," a voice yelled from over by the jungle gym. It was Dylan Shumack, hanging upside down by his knees with a bloody knife protruding from his chest. "Why don't you just kiss her already?"

"Shut up," Joey yelled back, but he didn't seem too bothered. "So, are we square?" he asked Madison.

"Yeah, we're square."

"Great. See you around, Mad-one," he said, and he clomped away in his oversized waders to join his best friend.

Watching him go, Madison wished for the millionth time that she and Alyssa hadn't gotten into that fight. It had been fun being best friends. Alyssa was so quirky and alive. The air seemed to crackle around her, which had made Madison experience the world in a totally different way.

But now everything sucked. She didn't have a best friend anymore, no one to laugh and talk with. And she didn't want to go back to hanging out with Olivia and Isabelle, even if she could.

It felt awkward. *She* felt awkward, like she no longer fit into her old skin. Maybe she never had.

Madison made her way across the playground, leaning forward into the wind that was hooting hard, sending gusts of leaves and dirt swirling into the air like miniature tornadoes.

A first-grade kid dressed as a scarecrow darted past, closely followed by a gleeful, green-faced witch. "I'm going to kiss you, Jonathan White, see if I don't!" she shrieked.

"Yikes," the scarecrow yelped, clutching his beat-up old hat and pretending to pick up speed, but Madison could tell that he wanted to get caught. He did a loop-the-loop around the tetherball pole, and just as the witch reached out, her lips puckered, he slipped down out of her grasp, scrambled on all fours until he got his balance, and then ran laughing, arms whirling like windmills as he disappeared around the side of the building.

Why had Dylan said that about Joey kissing her? Did Joey like her that way? Thinking about it made her stomach feel funny, sort of excited and repulsed at the same time.

Madison turned the corner. The wind was stronger here. She wrapped her arms tightly around her body. She probably should have worn a coat. She was cold, but still her footsteps slowed as she approached the rest of her class lining up outside their door. She was having doubts about the wisdom of her outfit.

"Oh my god, Maddie, what are you?" Olivia called out. She was wearing a long, tight, red-sequined dress, a short platinum-blond wig, a white feather boa, cherry red lipstick, and long dark false eyelashes with glitter on them.

"I'm a broken-slash-dead doll," Madison said. She tilted her head and did a couple of jerky dead-doll steps, which made Olivia and Isabelle shriek with laughter.

"You're crazy," Olivia chortled. "Who else would come up with something so bizarre?"

"And you guys are …?" Madison asked. It was clear that Olivia was some kind of fancy lady, but Isabelle was wearing baggy pants and a grungy sweater and had a camera slung around her neck.

"Well, I'm—"

"No," Isabelle said, slapping her hand over Olivia's mouth. "Make her guess."

"Okay," Olivia said, stepping forward and striking a glamorous pose.

"Hmm …" Madison said, squinting slightly. It didn't help. She still had no idea. "I give up."

"Miss Ashton … Miss Ashton!" Isabelle shouted, leaping into action, snapping pictures, the camera flashing. "Look this way ... Please. Give us a smile. Beautiful!"

"You don't *look* like Jessica Ashton," Sarah said to Olivia as she slipped in line behind them, pushing her smeary glasses back up on the bridge of her nose. She was wearing the same flowing Gryffindor robes she'd worn last year and the year before. "She's all curves and her hair is more natural looking and longer too."

"Oh, thank you for your valuable critique," Isabelle said, turning and defending her friend's outfit, giving Sarah a cold stare. "Who are *you*?" she asked, pretending confusion. "Harry Potter?"

"No," Sarah replied, unfazed. "I'm Hermione Granger, you dummy."

"Of course," Isabelle tittered. "Silly me. The glasses threw——" She obviously had something else pithy to say, but whatever she caught sight of over Sarah's shoulder had distracted her. "Oh my, look who's back," she murmured, giving Olivia a nudge.

Madison turned. It was Alyssa.

35
static

Madison felt a lurch of hope. Alyssa was a broken dead doll too! Granted, her costume wasn't so great. Actually it wasn't a costume at all. She was wearing her hoodie and her regular jeans with the ragged hole in the knee, but she also had on the makeup they'd talked about: the whitish-grey foundation, the red circle on her nose and each cheek, the rosebud mouth and black eyelashes. Her hair was in messy braids too, and she'd drawn a scar across her face. It wasn't as good as Madison's, though—just a black line with little railroad-track stitches—which was surprising. With Alyssa's mom being in television, Madison had figured that her scar would be scary real and that her outfit would be, too.

"Oh, Alyssa," Isabelle sang out from the back of the lineup. "Look over here. Madison's a dead doll too." It seemed like the entire class glanced from Madison to Alyssa and then back to Isabelle and Olivia, to see what they were going to say next.

"Twins," Olivia said. "How sweet. Of course," she continued, turning to do a slow pirouette, "*we* chose to be something truly great."

And as if by some invisible cue, Isabelle leapt into action again, her camera flashing. "Miss Ashton! Miss Ashton!" she screamed.

Alyssa froze, then her gaze slid over the posing twosome to land on Madison, who wanted to step forward and smile, be pals again, but something about the ferocious expression on Alyssa's face stopped her.

She thinks I told them, Madison realized in a panic. "I didn't—" she tried to say, but Isabelle cut her off.

"It's very odd, though," Isabelle said, her arm gesturing outward. "The two of you coming up with the same idea when everyone knows you aren't friends anymore. ESP perhaps? Or maybe …" She tapped her finger on her upper lip, pretending to be deep in thought. "… Maybe you saw Madison's brilliant costume, forgot to bring one of your own, and so you borrowed some makeup from a teacher and *copied* her?"

"Shut up, Isabelle," Madison managed to get

out. "Alyssa, listen, I didn't …" But it was too late. Alyssa had already disappeared around the corner of the building. "Why did you say that?" Madison demanded.

"We don't like her," Isabelle said, examining her nails. "She's stuck up and weird."

When the morning bell rang, Alyssa hadn't rejoined the lineup. She wasn't in the class-room when they filed in, either. Had she called Maximilian and left school again? Madison wouldn't have blamed her if she had. This was terrible. Alyssa *must* have thought that she'd told Olivia and Isabelle who her mother was and that they were all ganging up to make fun of her.

"Well, class, you look fantastic," Ms. Elliot said as she walked over to close the door, the long beads from her flapper outfit swaying and making a *chuusssh, chuusssh* noise.

"So do you, Ms. Elliot," Rocco said. Joey and Dylan snickered and elbowed each other, which caused Rocco's face to turn beet red. Everyone knew he had a hopeless crush on the teacher.

"Thank you, Rocco." Ms. Elliot smiled, reaching out to shut the door to the hall. "Oh, hello, there," she said, a little surprised as Alyssa darted under her arm and into the classroom.

Alyssa had her head tucked down, but even with her hair falling forward, Madison could see that she'd scrubbed her face clean. Only the faintest traces of makeup remained, and not for lack of trying, given how flushed her skin was from all that washing.

Madison heard Olivia and Isabelle whisper something, then Isabelle leaned forward and poked her in the shoulder with the eraser end of her pencil. Madison didn't turn around. She didn't want Alyssa to think she was gossiping or was at all okay with what they'd done. But Alyssa didn't even look in her direction. She didn't look at anyone. She just went to her seat, sat down with her arms crossed, and stared straight ahead, her chin jutted out and a defiant, who-cares look on her face.

"We're going to start off with science today," Ms. Elliot said, walking over to the dry-erase board.

"Science," Brian groaned. "But it's Halloween, Ms. Elliot."

"Be that as it may," Ms. Elliot answered. "It's my job to educate you, and educate you I will. Since we've completed our unit on plants, we are now moving on to electricity," she said, writing ELECTRICITY on the board with a blue marker.

"Electricity," Joey crowed, making his Christmas tree lights flash on and off.

"Yes, that *is* a very good example of electricity. Thank you, Joey, for the excellent demonstration. Now, as exciting as your costume is, I'm going to ask you to turn those lights off until a few minutes before recess."

"Aww, Ms. Elliot—" Joey started to protest.

"At which time," Ms. Elliot cut in, "I'd like you to share with us how you came up with such a unique idea, and explain to the class how it works."

Joey tried not to let on how pleased he was. "Sure, Ms. Elliot," he said, proudly reaching into his pouch and disconnecting the battery from the string of lights. "No problem."

"Thank you." Ms. Elliot turned back to the class. "Electricity has become an integral part of the way we live our lives. Without it we wouldn't be able to flick a switch to make the lights come on, our cars wouldn't start, many of us would be unable to cook our meals in our microwaves or ovens ..."

Madison glanced across the room to Alyssa, who was still staring straight ahead with her arms folded. Had she put the makeup on because she wanted to let bygones be bygones, too?

"Now, many people believe that Benjamin Franklin"—Ms. Elliot wrote his name on the board and underlined it—"was the father of electricity. This is an incorrect assumption. Benjamin Franklin did important research with regard to electricity and its properties. However, it was over two thousand years ago, around six hundred BCE, when the ancient Greeks discovered that if they rubbed fur on amber, it caused an attraction between the two objects ..."

If only Olivia and Isabelle hadn't dressed up as Jessica Ashton and a paparazzo, if only they hadn't been standing next to Madison and chosen that moment to be mean, maybe everything would have been okay with Alyssa by now. Madison felt slightly sick just thinking about it. If only she could get a chance to talk with Alyssa and sort out this whole misunderstanding.

"So, I thought it would be interesting to do a variation on those experiments that were carried out thousands of years ago. Unfortunately, I don't have a load of amber lying around. I do have, however ..." Ms. Elliot opened a drawer in her desk, pulled out a little brown paper bag, and dumped the contents on her desk. "Balloons," she said, picking one up and waving it in the air. "I brought black and orange ones, since it's Halloween. Now, I'd like you to break up into groups of three. Someone from each group will need to come up front to get a balloon and a worksheet. We're going to blow up the balloon, tie it, and then conduct several experiments to observe some of the properties of static electricity."

The class broke into excited chatter as they formed into groups.

This was her chance. Madison got up from her desk and started to make her way over to where Alyssa was standing when suddenly Dylan frog-hopped over his seat and banged right into her. "Ouch!" she said, rubbing her chin where his head had bashed it.

"Sorry about that," Dylan said, massaging his forehead.

"Dylan, please watch where you're going," Ms. Elliot called. "Are you all right, Madison?"

"Yes, thanks," Madison replied, stepping around Dylan. But it was too late—Alyssa was already in a group with Taylor and Grace.

"Where are you going, silly," Olivia said, tapping Madison on the shoulder. "We're over here."

Madison glanced around the room, hoping there was another cluster she could slip into, but everyone was already in groups. Madison sighed and turned to join Olivia and Isabelle. This day was becoming a real stinker.

36

short circuit

"She must be poor as dirt, always wearing that hoodie and those old ripped-up jeans," Olivia said, rubbing a blown-up black balloon on Isabelle's head.

"Maybe she likes them." Madison watched as Isabelle's hair started to rise and cling to the balloon.

"Oh, please," Isabelle snorted. "Who would like ratty old jeans like that?"

"And remember that time she came to school with paint splattered on her face?" Olivia giggled. "Doesn't the girl have a mirror?"

"And she is *way* too skinny," Isabelle added, her hand on her hip, her lips pursed. "Her family must starve her to death. She's like a walking skeleton. I don't know why she bothered putting Halloween makeup on. She didn't need a costume. Meet Alyssa Hawkins, the walking, breathing skeleton. I bet she's anorexic."

Madison felt herself getting mad. She wanted to say, *If Alyssa's family is sooo poor, then how come she lives in a mansion and has a cook, a housekeeper, and a chauffeur? Huh, Miss Know-It-All?* But she had pinky-sworn and would keep her promise. "I think," she said, trying to keep her voice neutral, "Lyssa wears those jeans because they're comfortable and she likes them." She glanced coolly at Isabelle's hair, which was now making snapping, crackling noises as more and more strands rose up and plastered themselves on the balloon. Madison bent over and wrote down her observations in her science binder.

"Not likely," Olivia chimed in. "Besides, why are you sticking up for her? You aren't even friends anymore."

"Because," Madison said, not looking up from her notes, "she's nice and she's decent and just because we aren't hanging out doesn't mean I'm going to trash-talk her—"

"You are such a wuss," Isabelle sneered. "She dumps you, is rude to the world, copies your Halloween outfit—"

"We came up with the broken-dead-doll idea together!" Madison yelled, banging her pencil down, suddenly fed up. "And it belonged to Alyssa more than it belonged to me. Why are you being so mean about her? What has she ever done that was so horrible to you? Huh?!"

There was silence in the room. Madison could hear her heart thumping loudly in her chest. Olivia and Isabelle were staring at her as if she'd grown two heads, but Madison didn't dare look away from their faces, because it was clear by the lack of noise in the class that everybody else must be staring as well.

"Is everything okay there, girls?" Madison heard Ms. Elliot ask.

"Everything is fine." Isabelle turned and gave the teacher one of her I'm-such-a-sweet-little-angel smiles. "Isn't it, Madison?"

"Uh ... huh ..." Madison nodded, feeling sick, her face on fire.

"Well, then, try to keep the noise level down."

"Okay, Ms. Elliot," Isabelle said.

Everyone started murmuring as they went back to their experiments.

"Why did you invite her to join us?" Isabelle asked Olivia, as if Madison had ceased to exist.

Olivia shrugged. "She used to be fun."

"Not anymore. Well," Isabelle said and sighed, flinging her arm around Olivia's shoulders, "we shall have to be brave, hold our noses, finish this assignment, and never make the mistake of inviting *her* to do anything with *us* ever again."

"I agree," Olivia said, giving Madison a baleful look.

They finished the experiment in silence. When they were done, the three of them went to their separate desks and waited for the rest of the class to finish having fun.

failed truancy

"Come on, Maddie, get up."

Madison could feel her little sister's butt land on her bed and start bouncing up and down. She could hear the soles of Gina's shiny black shoes slapping the floor lightly. "Go away," she muttered, tucking down into her covers, her eyes squeezed shut.

"Mommy knocked on the door a long time ago," Gina announced. "I've already washed my face, brushed my hair, and gotten dressed. You're going to be late for school."

"I'm not going."

The bouncing movement stilled. "What?"

"I'm *not* going to school."

There was a long pause while Gina absorbed that statement. "Why?"

"None of your stupid business," Madison

said through clenched teeth. "Go away." There was another long pause. Madison didn't need to open her eyes to know that Gina was staring at her. "Scat!"

"Mom!" Gina bellowed as she jumped off Madison's bed and hop-skipped out of the room and down the hall. "Madison won't get out of bed, and she told me to scat, and she's not dressed or anything, and we're going to be late for school!"

"Madison?" She heard the brisk click of her mother's work shoes coming down the hall, accompanied by her little sister's prancing feet.

"Great," she groaned, slinking further under her covers. Her mother's footsteps crossed the room. Madison felt the bed shift as her mother sat down beside her.

"Honey, are you all right?"

Madison shook her head. She wasn't all right. Nothing was right. Nothing would be right ever again.

"Honey, look at me." Madison reluctantly turned and opened her eyes. Her mom placed the back of her hand against Madison's forehead and frowned. "You don't have a fever."

"Mom, please, I don't want to go to school."

"Why?"

"That's what I said," Gina chirped, shaking her head solemnly, "but she wouldn't answer me."

"Gina, go to the kitchen and eat your breakfast. I'll join you in a minute."

"I don't—"

"Hop to it," their mom said, giving her younger daughter a stern, no-nonsense look. "And shut the door behind you."

Gina sighed. "Why do I *always* miss the *good* conversations?" she moaned, reluctantly leaving the room and closing the door with a thump.

"What's going on, sweetie?" her mother asked, the train-track furrows deepening above the bridge of her nose. "Why don't you want to go to school? You've always loved it and—"

"I just don't." Unwanted tears sprang to Madison's eyes. She had to squeeze her lips together tight, because the desire to tell her mom everything, to let it all spill out, was almost overwhelming. It would be such a relief to discuss the difficulties of the last few weeks and ask her advice, but Madison couldn't. "Why do I have to go?"

"Well, it's the law. Everyone goes to school."

"You could home-school me. People do it all the time."

"Sweetheart," her mom sighed, taking a quick glance down at her wristwatch. "It's just not practical. Both your father and I work and I'm going to be late if you don't get a move on."

"Daddy's only part-time, he could do it."

"Your father is looking for work—"

"Then maybe Grandpa could teach me—"

"Madison," her mother interrupted, a snap of impatience coming to the forefront. "*What* is going on?"

"Nothing! Okay." Madison found herself yelling, dashing away the angry tears that had spilled from her eyes. "Nothing is going on." She flung the covers off and leapt out of bed. "Everything is fine. Hunky-dory. I'll get dressed for school like a good little girl," she spat out. She could feel her face all screwed up and bitter, saw the hurt look in her mom's eyes, but she didn't care. She stormed to her dresser, threw her pyjamas off, and yanked on a pair of jeans and a shirt. "There," Madison said, turning to glare at her mother while she swiped a brush through her hair. "I'm ready." She tossed the brush back on her dresser, stomped to the door, and swung it open. "Now you won't be late for your precious work. I hope you're happy," she said and then slammed the door hard behind her.

38
surprise

"I knew you'd have to go to school," Gina said, scampering along beside Madison at a half-run so she wouldn't get left behind. "You should have listened to me. Then you wouldn't have made Mommy sad."

"Shut up," Madison said, but there wasn't any bite to it. She was too weary for that. They turned into the schoolyard. Madison felt a tug on her coat sleeve. She looked down. Gina was looking up at her sorrowfully.

"Maddie ..."

"What?"

"I'm so sorry you had a difficult morning." And the way Gina said it, so sincere and heartfelt, made the hard knot that was clenched inside Madison's chest soften.

"It's okay, kiddo."

"Would you like a hug?" Gina cocked her head to the side like a bright-eyed robin. "It'll make you feel better."

"Sure, okay," Madison said, even though it was embarrassing. Some things were more important—and if Gina felt the need to hug her, so be it. Madison bent down and Gina flung her arms around her neck and squeezed tight.

"I love you sooo much!" Gina said, her voice a strangled growl as she planted a wet kiss on Madison's cheek.

"Ooooh!" Madison heard a boy whoop. "Kissing at school. Oooh."

"Get lost, doofus," Madison called over her shoulder, not even bothering to turn around. "Hop up," she told her little sister. "I'll give you a piggyback ride." Gina scrambled onto her back. "Hang on tight," Madison instructed, and then took off in a gallop-trot that made Gina shriek with laughter, her dangling feet bumping against Madison's thighs. By the time she deposited a giggling Gina at her kindergarten doorway, Madison was pretty winded, but it was worth it to see Gina's big beaming smile.

The warning bell rang. "See you after school," Madison said, straightening up, stretching out her back.

"Wait! I almost forgot." Gina squatted down

and started rummaging in her backpack. "Aha . . . here it is." She pulled out a crumpled envelope. "Mommy wanted me to give this to you." Madison stared at the envelope. From where she was standing, she could see the official, machine-printed address in the left-hand corner. "It came in the mail this morning for your friend Alyssa," Gina continued, pressing the envelope in Madison's hand. "The post office must have made a mistake."

"Thank you, Gina," Madison said, her voice sounding gruff in her ears.

"Okay, bye-bye. See you later," Gina said, waving both hands in the air.

"See you later." Madison turned to go.

"That's my big sister!" she heard Gina say to a dark-haired girl with a polka-dot bow in her hair. The proud tone in her voice made Madison smile, despite her worry about how she was going to get this important envelope to Alyssa, who was avoiding her like the plague.

"You're lucky," the dark-haired girl replied, sounding sort of wistful. "I wish I had a——"

Madison didn't hear the rest of her sentence, just the wind in her ears as she jogged around the corner of the brick building, her mind spinning. What was she supposed to do? Run Alyssa down and tackle her? Madison shook her head, folding the envelope and stuffing it in her pocket. She would find a way. She had to. The information in this envelope went beyond hurt feelings or fights. This had to do with who Alyssa's father was. Alyssa had a right to know that, even if they weren't friends anymore.

The tail end of her class was entering the school. Madison put on a burst of speed and managed to grab the heavy outside door and slip inside before it swung shut. The air in the hall was nice and warm on her cheeks and smelled of polished floors, old apple cores, and books.

As she followed Dylan into the classroom, yesterday's humiliation in science class came flooding back. She kept her gaze on the floor so she wouldn't have to look at anybody. Dylan's left tennis shoe was untied and the oversized lace flopped when he walked. It must have been dragging on the ground for a while because it was pretty muddy.

Madison turned down the aisle and past three sets of desks to her own. She sat in her seat, the envelope crackling in her back pocket. She unbuttoned her jacket and hung it on the back of her chair. No way was she going to make the trek to her hook and cubby in the cloakroom. She didn't look in Olivia or Isabelle's direction. She could hear their whispered giggles, though.

Madison propped her elbows on the desk and leaned forward on them, letting her head fall forward a little so she could casually sneak a peek behind her without being too obvious. She could see a splash of colour, the lilac of Alyssa's hoodie.

Alyssa was here. Somehow, someway, Madison would get that envelope to her. Actually, if she got up right now, as if she'd decided to hang her jacket in her cubby after all, she could sneak the envelope into Alyssa's backpack.

Madison stood and started to lift up her jacket.

"Good morning, class," she heard Ms. Elliot say.

Too late. Madison replaced her jacket and sat back down.

"Good morning, Ms. Elliot," everyone replied.

At recess she would hang back, go to the bathroom, give everyone time to clear out of the classroom, and then sneak back in. It was a good plan. Madison took a deep breath and let it out. Math was first up today. She reached inside her desk to get out her textbook; no need to wait for Ms. Elliot to tell her what she already knew.

Her hand bumped against something. It surprised her. *That* wasn't in her desk yesterday.

Did she make a mistake? Sit in the wrong desk? She could feel her cheeks heat up. Madison glanced around, keeping her head tilted down. No, it *was* her desk.

"If you could please take out your math books and turn to page sixty-four," Ms. Elliot was saying.

Madison tipped her body to the side so she could see partly into her desk and gingerly reached in again. Her hand closed around the object, and she pulled it out. Her breath caught in her throat. She was looking at a genuine Rawlings PROSCM20B Pro Preferred Series catcher's mitt—and taped to the palm was a folded piece of paper. Madison opened it and read,

> I'm sorry I was such an idiot. I've been thinking about it a lot and realized that you must have meant you didn't want to lie to your family. Of course you can tell them. Do you forgive me?
>
> P.S. Thank you for standing up for me in science yesterday. You're the best friend I ever had.

"Oh my," she whispered, her hand flying up to her mouth. She spun around in her seat and there was Alyssa, watching her with a tentative half-smile on her face.

Madison kept the note and the beautiful tan mitt with its dark-brown, full-grain leather laces below her desk so as not to attract attention. She tipped it toward Alyssa. "For me?" she mouthed, still hardly able to believe it, her heart still pounding erratically in her chest.

Alyssa nodded, her eyes sparkling.

A surge of joy shot through Madison's body, making her tingle from head to toe. She wanted to dance around the room, race over and give Alyssa the biggest hug, whirl the precious glove over her head like a cowboy in the Wild West, and shout at the top of her lungs, *Wahhoooo! We're best friends again!* But this was private. "I have something for you too," she mouthed. "We'll talk at recess."

Alyssa nodded, still smiling big.

"Now, is everyone on page sixty-four?" Ms. Elliot continued.

Madison carefully placed her new catcher's mitt back into her desk with the biggest, goofiest grin on her face. Then both girls turned back toward the teacher, got out their math books, and opened them.

39
birth certificate

Neither one of them spoke, walking fast toward the old tree just beyond the jungle gym and swings. That's how it was with them: they didn't have to ask where the other one wanted to go, they just knew. It felt to Madison like the world was right again. There was a happy thrumming inside her chest mixed with a tiny dash of nervousness. What was she going to say? Would Alyssa accept her apology?

They reached the tree and Madison turned. "I am *so* sorry," she said. But the funny thing was, Alyssa was saying "I am *so* sorry" too. Same exact words at the same exact time. The surprise of it made them both start laughing. And that was that—it was as if the argument had never happened.

"I missed you," Alyssa said.

"Me too," Madison replied. The two of them, standing there, smiled at each other.

Alyssa had the envelope Madison had given her in her hand. She looked at it, her expression turning serious. "I feel kind of shaky," she said. "It's hard to believe that after all these years, I'm finally going to know who my father is."

"Do you think you'll try to meet him?" Madison asked.

Alyssa caught her lower lip between her teeth. "I don't know," she said. "I hadn't thought that far ahead." She looked pale.

"You aren't going to faint, are you?"

Alyssa shook her head.

"Maybe you should sit down?"

"I'm okay, really," Alyssa said, but her eyes seemed darker, larger in her face. It reminded Madison of the expression Gina would get when she had to go to the dentist or was watching a scary show.

"Just do it," Madison said, giving Alyssa a nudge. "Open it up."

"You're right." Alyssa took a deep breath. "Here goes." She slid her finger under the flap and lifted it up. The envelope ripped. She reached inside and withdrew the birth certificate. Madison noticed that Alyssa's fingers were shaking slightly as she unfolded the document and read it. She blinked. Then she seemed to be reading it again, a faint frown line forming on her forehead.

"What?" Madison asked. "What does it say?"

Alyssa looked up from the birth certificate, her eyes blank, her arms falling to her side, the document loose in her fingers. "Nothing," she said.

"What do you mean, nothing?"

"Nothing," Alyssa repeated, a snap of impatience creeping in. "It says nothing."

"Let me see." Madison reached out her hand. For a second she thought Alyssa wasn't going to let her, but then Alyssa blew out a puff of air and handed the birth certificate to her. Madison scanned it. Alyssa was right. There was Alyssa's name, where she was born, and the date she was born. Beside *Maiden Name of Mother* was Jessica Diane Hawkins. Beside *Birthplace of Mother* was Seattle, Washington. But both *Name of Father* and *Birthplace of Father* were blank.

Madison looked at Alyssa, who was standing with her arms crossed, wrapped tight around her body as if she was cold and would never get warm again. Madison put her arm around her shoulder. "I'm sorry, Alyssa," she said. "I'm so sorry." She didn't know what else to do. Her friend was in so much pain, and she had no way of making it better.

Alyssa didn't say anything, just stood there, faint tremors running through her, her breath shaky.

"It's not fair," she finally whispered. "It's just not fair."

Madison nodded. It *wasn't* fair. "I think," she said, working it out as she spoke, "that you should talk to your mom."

"I have!"

"No. Really talk to her. Tell her how much it means to you. That you need to know. That you feel ... I don't know ..."

"Unfinished?" Alyssa said.

"Yeah. Unfinished. Like a part of you isn't acknowledged."

Alyssa straightened, her gaze searching Madison's face. Then she nodded. "Okay," she said. "Will you come with me?"

40
permission

"Please, Mom," Madison said. "It's—"

"Are you calling from home?" Madison's mom asked. "There seems to be a lot of static on the line. Ask Daddy to look at the phone— maybe if he jiggles the cord a bit, checks the connection ..."

"I can't. I'm at school."

"You're at school?" There was a pause. Madison's mom cleared her throat. "And you're talking on ...?"

Madison could feel the cold imprint of the chain-link fence against her back. Alyssa was standing beside her with a hopeful look on her face, her fingers crossed. Gina was perched on an empty bike rack pretending it was a pony ride. "I ... um ... borrowed Alyssa's cell phone—"

"You know how I feel about cell phones, Madison."

"Yes, Mom, but this was——"

A loud squawk came from behind them. The fence gave a violent shake. Madison and Alyssa spun around, startled. There were Joey, Dylan, Brian, and Rocco clambering on the fence, fingers poking through the holes as if they were desperate inmates in prison. "Help! Lemme out!" Joey yelled. So of course Dylan, Brian, and Rocco followed suit. "Bust us outta here!" "Can't take this prison no longer!" Now they were all shaking the fence with huge grins on their faces.

Alyssa tried to shoo them away, but that just made them gyrate and wail even more.

"What *is* that?" Madison's mom sounded worried.

"Nothing, Mom." Madison stuck her tongue out at Joey and moved away from the fence. "Just some dumb boys at school," she said loudly, to make sure they heard her. She hoisted Gina off the bike rack and the three girls walked around the side of the school, the boys' wails receding into the distance. "Please, Mom. Say yes. I know Dad was planning a big yard cleanup, but it's really important for me to be with Alyssa tonight. She needs me."

Madison's mom sighed heavily, which usually meant she was on the cusp of relenting.

"We can do the cleanup when I get back," Madison said. "And I'll work really hard and I won't complain."

Alyssa crowded her mouth close to the phone. "Please, Mrs. Stokes," she said. "I'll come too. I've never done yardwork before, but I'm a fast learner and a hard worker."

Gina hopped up and down, arms flapping like a baby bird trying to fly. "Me too!" she chimed. "Me too! And I won't complain either."

"Okay, okay …" Her mom laughed, and the sound of it warmed Madison's heart. She could just imagine her mom taking a step back, hands in the air, smiling and shaking her head slightly. "You can sleep over at Alyssa's. We'll push the yard cleanup to Sunday."

"Yes!" Madison said, giving Alyssa the thumbs-up and watching as she leapt around and around, pumping her fists triumphantly in the air. "Thanks Mom. I love you."

"I love you too," her mom said.

Madison handed the cell phone back to Alyssa. "Okay," she said, smiling down at her kid sister, "let's get you home."

courage

"You're falling asleep," Alyssa said, a suppressed laugh in her voice.

"No, I'm not," Madison protested, jerking her head upright and forcing her heavy eyelids to open. "I'm awake. I'm awake." She smothered a large yawn behind her hand. "What do you want to do? Watch another video? Play some more Yahtzee?"

Bong … bong … bong … bong … Madison glanced at the glass clock on the mantel. *Bong … bong … bong … bong …* Oh my! *Bong … bong … bong …* It was eleven o'clock. No wonder she was tired. She looked over at a weary-eyed Alyssa. "What time does your mom usually get home?"

"Don't know," Alyssa said with a shrug. "It's always different. Sometimes she gets picked up for work at five a.m. and doesn't get home till after midnight. Other times, she might get called to the set at eight in the morning, do one scene, and then be home in time for lunch. It all depends on what they're shooting that day and how many scenes she's in."

"Must be hard to plan things."

"Yeah," Alyssa said. "She's always having to cancel on me. It's not her fault, though. The worst is when she has night shooting, because then, even though she's home during the day, I don't get to see her because she's trying to sleep, and I have to be super quiet so I won't wake her."

"They actually shoot at night?"

"Yeah, all through the night. She's always super exhausted when she's doing a night shoot, and the conditions can be pretty bad. Everyone's tired and grouchy and it can be really cold. When that happens, not only does she have to act in whatever the scene is, but she has to pretend she's not freezing as well.

"She was doing a night shoot last year in Montana. It was three o'clock in the morning when a freak snowstorm blew in. She was wearing a sleeveless summer dress and sandals, and between each take, the prop guys were out there with blowtorches, melting all the snow around the bench she was sitting on."

"Wow, she must have been freezing."

"Yeah, and to make matters worse, the cinematographer said he could see puffs of steam coming out of her mouth, and so she had to have an ice cube in her mouth and then spit it out right before the cameras rolled.

"She came back to the hotel and crawled in bed with me. I got all the blankets from her bed and mine, even the spare blanket from the hotel closet, and piled them all on top of her, but it took a really long time for her body to stop shaking."

Both girls were silent for a moment.

"Pretty glamorous, huh?" Alyssa said.

She said it like it was a joke, but Madison felt bad anyway. It must suck for Alyssa to come home from school and not know whether she'd see her mom before she went to bed. And on top of that, not to know who her dad was?

Hopefully, the talk with Alyssa's mom would go well. A flutter of nerves rushed through Madison's body. It had seemed so simple in the schoolyard to say "Why don't you talk to her?" It had felt so straightforward, but as the day wore on and evening turned into night, Madison had gotten more and more anxious. What if she'd given Alyssa bad advice? Just because *her* mom was easy to talk to didn't mean that Alyssa's mom would be. What if Alyssa's mom got mad? Or yelled at them? Or decided that Madison was a troublemaker for even suggesting that Alyssa ask her for the truth? What if she forbade Alyssa to be friends with her anymore?

Madison swallowed hard. "Um ... I'm going to get some water from the kitchen. Do you want some?"

"No thanks." Alyssa stretched her arms out and then slid down so that her head was resting on the arm of the sofa. "Do you need help finding the glasses?" she asked, snuggling down a bit more with a sleepy yawn.

"You rest," Madison said. "I'll find them." She walked through the dining room and into the kitchen, the big white doors swinging shut behind her.

She'd walked through the kitchen before with Alyssa, but she hadn't taken it in. They'd been on their way out to the beach, Berta had been mopping the floor, and Madison hadn't known which way to look. She didn't want Berta to think she was staring at her cleaning someone else's floor, so she'd kept her eyes forward on Alyssa's back.

The kitchen was empty now. Most of the lights were out. It was very quiet. Huge, too, with tons of cupboards and gleaming black-and-white tiles on the floor. The countertops were white marble, and so was the island in the middle. There were three tall chrome and white leather chairs at the island and a vase of fresh flowers sitting on top. And there were two sets of sinks! Oh my! Madison turned around and saw the stove. It was gas with six burners and some kind of grill thing. Her dad would die to have a stove like that.

And somehow, the thought of her dad sobered Madison up. Yes, the kitchen was pretty, but it didn't make up for the emptiness of the place. It was as though the kitchen was *pretending* to be a kitchen.

Madison suddenly got an image of the kitchen in her home. It was a cozy place to be—the place where her family shared meals and stories and cooked and cleaned. It was the heart of the house, really.

She opened a few cupboards, but couldn't find glasses. So she went over to one of the sinks, turned the water on, and drank out of the faucet. Then she wiped the faucet off with a tea towel. At home she wouldn't have bothered, but here everything was so pristine and shiny that she wanted to make sure she didn't leave any mess.

When Madison got back to the living room, Alyssa was asleep on the sofa, one arm flung up over her head. *Ha!* Madison thought. *And you were teasing me about being sleepy.*

She glanced at the clock. Eleven eighteen. She'd never stayed up this late before. She sat down in the big white armchair to wait.

42
the talk

Madison woke up discombobulated, not sure for a second where she was. Silvery moonlight flooded through the big plate-glass windows. There was a rattle of keys at the front door, and then she remembered. She wished she'd sat on the sofa because then she could have reached out and gently nudged Alyssa awake, but it was too late to move now.

Alyssa's mom came through the door and dropped her keys back in her purse. She slipped out of her coat and hung it in the closet, rolling her shoulders as though they were a bit tense. She seemed like any other mom coming home after a long day at work.

Madison didn't know what to do. She'd never been in a situation like this before. Should she say hello? But then what? Alyssa's mom would want to know why they weren't in bed, and Madison couldn't tell her. And of course she couldn't ask about Alyssa's dad—that was for Alyssa to do. If Madison asked, Miss Ashton would think she was being rude or nosy or that she wanted to sell the scoop to *The Hollywood Insider*.

No. The best thing she could do was keep pretending to be asleep. She'd wake Alyssa up once her mom went to her bedroom. Madison watched Miss Ashton through her eyelashes as she started up the stairs, but suddenly she stopped. It reminded Madison of when she'd be hiking with her grandpa and they'd come across a wild deer or rabbit. Miss Ashton looked like that—like she was suddenly aware she wasn't the only creature in the field.

She slowly turned her head. When she saw the girls, the tension seemed to ease, although it seemed to Madison that maybe Miss Ashton could tell she was watching her. So she quickly squeezed her eyelids shut all the way and breathed shallowly, keeping her body still, so still. She could hear Miss Ashton's footsteps as she walked back down the stairs. She could hear her approach the sofa, the soft muted squeak of the sofa springs and fabric as she sat. Madison cracked her eyelids open a tiny bit. Miss Ashton was sitting beside Alyssa. She still had her movie makeup on. And she was gazing at Alyssa with such love and longing in her eyes that Madison almost felt embarrassed to be present in such a private moment. Still, she couldn't just pop up and say, *Hey, I'm awake. If you'll just hold everything while I scamper out of the room.*

Alyssa's mom smoothed a strand of hair out of Alyssa's face then bent over and placed a tender kiss on her forehead.

Alyssa woke. "Hi Mom," she said, still half asleep.

Alyssa's mom smiled. "You funny little sprogglet, what are you doing up? Why didn't you go to bed?"

Alyssa pushed herself to a seated position. "I uh ..." She cleared her throat, seemingly unable to lift her gaze further than the second button on her mother's blouse. "I wanted to ask you something ... Something important."

"All right," her mom said. "What is it?"

"I want to know ..." Alyssa swallowed. She was wringing her hands.

Say it, Madison whispered in her head. *Just say it.*

Alyssa straightened and looked her mom in the face. "I want to know"—her voice was stronger now—"who my father is."

"Oh honey," Alyssa's mom said and sighed.

She looked suddenly weary and sort of sad. "What does it matter? I'm your mother and I love you more than life itself. Isn't that enough?"

"No, it's not. I *need* to know, Mom. It's important to me." Alyssa was looking back at her hands again, and Madison could tell that even though Alyssa was trying to stay calm, she was crying. "I even sent away for my birth certificate," she said, picking up the envelope on the coffee table and holding it out to her mom. "But when it came back, his name ..." Alyssa was sobbing hard now. "His name wasn't on it ..."

"Oh baby," Alyssa's mom said, scooping her daughter onto her lap, rocking her gently. "I'm so sorry. I had no idea."

Madison shut her eyes, but Alyssa's sadness was washing over her in great waves and she could feel her own tears escaping from beneath her eyelids.

"All right now," Alyssa's mom crooned. "It's okay, honey. I didn't know it was so important to you. How about we go into the kitchen and I'll make us some nice cups of cocoa and you can ask me whatever you want. Hmm?"

"Okay," Alyssa said.

Madison heard the two of them get off the sofa. She was glad Alyssa was finally going to know. She heard them walking toward her chair.

She heard them stop. She felt a hand alight gently on her head. "Would you like some cocoa too?" she heard Alyssa's mom say. Madison froze. What should she do? She was supposed to be asleep— should she pretend she didn't hear? No. That was dumb. It was obvious that Alyssa's mom knew she was awake.

Madison opened her eyes, feeling kind of embarrassed. Alyssa and her mom were standing beside her, arms around each other, snuggled in.

"Oh, thanks, but I was thinking maybe I'll go upstairs to bed." She glanced at Alyssa to make sure it was okay. Alyssa gave her a slight smile and nod. Madison smiled back, then yawned big. "I'm awfully tired."

Alyssa's mom chuckled. So maybe Madison wasn't cut out to be an actress, but no one said anything. And she went upstairs, vibrating with curiosity, to wait.

43
new beginnings

The next morning, Alyssa and Madison sat on the patio at a little table that had been set up with a white tablecloth and another vase of fresh flowers. Tall glasses of orange juice, ice water, plates, and silverware had already been laid out for them. It all looked really pretty and fancy, but Madison was getting used to it. It was just the way things were done at Alyssa's house.

Alyssa finally knew who her father was. When she'd come upstairs last night after her talk with her mom, her face was glowing. She had crawled in bed, so happy. She told Madison that her dad was Josh Lowe, but that he didn't know. That nobody knew, nobody but her mom and now Alyssa and Madison too. And then Alyssa had fallen asleep, but Madison couldn't— her mind was spinning from the news.

When they woke up, Madison felt shy. It didn't make sense. She already knew that Alyssa's mom was Jessica Ashton, so why did it throw her for such a loop to find out Alyssa's father was none other than Josh Lowe, the world-famous heartthrob with the charismatic smile and tousled golden hair? There wasn't a bigger male movie star in the whole wide world. Even Madison's *mom* thought he was a hunk. But still, that shouldn't change how she looked at her friend. Alyssa was just Alyssa, same as before.

She should say something, and not just sit there tongue-tied. "Do you feel different?" Madison asked. "Knowing?"

"Yeah. A bit," Alyssa said.

The wind blew a strand of hair across Madison's face. She brushed it back behind her ears. "You look sort of like him."

"You think?"

"Yeah." Madison nodded. "Around the eyes, same colour." That was better. Now that they were chatting, she was feeling more normal, more like a friend.

"You know," Alyssa said, "it feels kind of silly to have gone through the trouble of getting my birth certificate when all I had to do was ask." She shook her head and smiled at Madison. "I never would have done it if it weren't for you."

"Oh," Madison said, embarrassed but pleased. "That's what friends are for."

Alyssa's mom was in the kitchen making pancakes. Apparently she'd never made them before, because through the window, they could see Berta fluttering around behind her, bringing her ingredients, wiping up spills.

"Have you ever met him?"

"No."

"Do you think you will?"

Alyssa thought about it, squinting in the sunlight, looking out over the ocean. "I don't know," she finally said. "If I did, I don't think I'd tell him he was my father."

Looking a little frazzled, Alyssa's mom came out from the kitchen carrying a plate full of pancakes, Berta trotting behind her with the syrup and butter. "Ta ... dah!" Alyssa's mom said as she placed the pancakes in the middle of the table and took her seat. "I can't vouch for how good they are," she said with a smile. "But now it can never be said that your mother didn't ever make you pancakes!"

The pancakes didn't look like any pancakes Madison had ever seen. Her dad made the best buttermilk pancakes in the world, golden brown all over, the outside with a slight bit of crisp, the inside moist and fluffy. But these pancakes that Alyssa's mom made? Oh my.

Madison blinked, swallowed. "Wow. Thanks," she said. It was a choice between pale, under-cooked pancakes or ones that were a little burnt. Alyssa took two and passed the plate to Madison, who gingerly speared one and put it on her plate.

She held the plate out to Alyssa's mom, but Jessica Ashton waved her off. "Oh, no," she said. "My pancake-eating days are long gone. Have to watch my girlish figure." She laughed, took a sip of her coffee, and leaned back in her chair.

Alyssa was tucking into the pancakes as if they were really good. Madison put some butter and syrup on hers. She cut a piece, stuck it into her mouth, and chewed. Even though her pancake was a little charred on the outside, it was kind of doughy in the middle.

"Are they okay?" Alyssa's mom asked.

Madison looked up. Alyssa's mom was watching them over the rim of her coffee cup, her eyes a little anxious. *Wow*, Madison thought. *She's nervous.*

"Oh yes," Madison said with a nod, putting an enthusiastic smile on her face.

"Are they *okay*?" Alyssa said, cheeks still full, snagging another pancake off the plate. "Are you kidding me? They're fantastic! These are the best pancakes I've ever tasted!" And Madison could tell that she really meant it, too.

"Oh good," Alyssa's mom said, her body seeming to relax. "I'm glad."

Alyssa ate five pancakes. Five! Madison managed to force down one and a half. The orange juice, however, was delicious. When she asked what kind it was, Miss Ashton said it was "freshly squeezed." Madison was going to see if she could convince her mom to buy that kind.

After Alyssa had eaten her fill, she put down her fork, dabbed her mouth with her napkin, and turned to Madison. "My mom and I were talking about it last night, and we were thinking that when Max takes you home today, we could go with you and I could introduce my mom to your parents. That is, if it's all right with you ...?"

Madison looked at Alyssa, her eyes wide. "Really? Are you sure?"

Alyssa nodded, a big grin on her face. Madison glanced at Miss Ashton and sure enough, she nodded too.

"That would be," Madison said, turning back to Alyssa, her heart, her eyes flooding with joy, "the best thing ever."

acknowledgments

I would like to thank Laura Langlie for her tireless support and input. She is an author's dream agent, and I am lucky enough to have access to her wisdom and insight, not just with my manuscripts and the professional side of things, but also on the human-life side. One couldn't have a better guardian angel.

My thanks as well to my talented editor, Lynne Missen, for her thoughtful, smart editorial comments and questions that uncovered layers and textures I didn't know were missing. You made this book so much better.

There are many others without whose support and hard work this book would not exist. These are the people who laboured behind the scenes and made *A Taste of Heaven* all that it could be. A huge thanks to Sandy Slater, production coordinator; Sandra Tooze, senior production editor; Karen Alliston, copyeditor; Catherine Dorton, proofreader; Lisa Jager, who designed the exquisite cover; B. J. Weckerle, who did the lovely interior design and formatting; Helen Smith, for her assistance; Sebastian Fabal, who helped me obtain copyright permission; and Vimala Jeevanandam and the entire Penguin Group sales force who worked hard to get my book into the hands of readers.

Speaking of readers, many thanks to all of you for the support you have given me and my books throughout the years. It is you that I write for. I am so happy that you have taken me and my characters into your hearts.

I'd also like to thank the booksellers, librarians, and teachers for your tireless support and championing of authors like me, and for the matchmaking you do, day in and day out, finding the right book for the right reader.

I'd like to thank my sisters, Jenny and Becky, and my children, Emily, Will, David, and his lovely wife, Amy. I am a better person for having you in my life.

And last but not least, my eternal gratitude to my husband, Don, who cheers me up when I am down. Who believes in me and shores me up when I have lost courage and feel small. Who comforts me when my heart is breaking. And dances and celebrates my successes as generously, as joyously, as if they were his own. I know how lucky I am to have you in my life, and I count my blessing each and every day.